all these lives

all these lives

all these lives

Sarah Wylie

Margaret Ferguson Books
Farrar Straus Giroux
New York

Farrar Straus Giroux Books for Young Readers
175 Fifth Avenue, New York 10010

Distributed in Canada by D&M Publishers, Inc.
Printed in the United States of America
Designed by Roberta Pressel
First edition, 2012
1   2   3   4   5   6   7   8   9   10

macteenbooks.com

Library of Congress Cataloging-in-Publication Data
Wylie, Sarah.
    All these lives / Sarah Wylie. — 1st ed.
        p.   cm.
    Summary: Convinced that she has nine lives after cheating death twice as a child,
sixteen year-old Dani tries to forfeit her remaining lives in hopes of saving her twin sister,
Jena, whose leukemia is consuming their family.
    ISBN 978-0-374-30208-5 (hardcover)
    ISBN 978-1-4299-5495-2 (e-book)
    [1. Near-death experiences—Fiction.   2. Sick—Fiction.   3. Cancer—Fiction.
4. Sisters—Fiction.   5. Twins—Fiction.   6. Family life—Fiction.]   I. Title.

PZ7.W97765All 2012
[Fic]—dc23

                                                                                2011030779

To my family

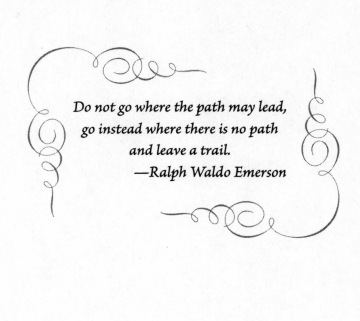

Do not go where the path may lead,
go instead where there is no path
and leave a trail.
—Ralph Waldo Emerson

Prologue

This is how it feels to die: It starts from outside and works its way in. Your cuticles, the tips of your fingers. Fire under your nails that spreads into your bones, burning and freezing everything it comes into contact with. Your arms, your ankles, your teeth, your knees, your stomach, and the place where your heart should be.

Your heart is always the last to go. One hundred irregular beats per minute, and then zero.

But that's just the start. The start of dying.

This is the rest.

nine

eight

seven

1

Once upon a time, my mother used to sleep through the night. So did I. Like so much else, our sleeping patterns were almost identical. We flung ourselves across our beds, sleeping through storms and hurricanes and car alarms and darkness, and waking up to a trail of sunlight filtering in, with the world still on its axis, still turning, the way we'd left it. She hasn't slept like that in seven months.

Now, she wakes up around two in the morning, as if to get a head start on all those elements. Or maybe she's figured out that the world tilts slightly when we sleep, and she gets up to watch it and try to pull it back in place.

I just lie there when I'm awake, trying to stay silent and hidden.

I'm sure my dad is aware that she barely sleeps, but it's not like he can get up and keep watch with her since he has to go to work in the morning.

None of us knows exactly what she does when she wakes up. Maybe she gets on her knees and holds vigil since she realized she believed in God the day my twin sister was diagnosed with leukemia. Or maybe she goes on the computer to look up cures. I personally think she's practicing some weird voodoo technique where she transfers all the cancer from Jena into her own body, so it can eat away at her cells and make her shriveled and ugly, and we can watch her die instead.

Once upon a time—back when she still slept—I didn't take my mother seriously. She would tell the same story over and over again. Tires squealing, flying through air, shattered glass, crushed metal. We were under crushed metal. Her and me.

She and I.

I was three months old when the accident happened. We were out of milk or something, and my mother asked Dad to watch Jena, while she took me out with her. Mom and I were just leaving the grocery store when a pickup truck ran into our car, destroying it.

We should have died.

I've never known what was more significant: the fact that we both survived, or the fact that she picked me.

I've heard the story so many times it feels like my memory instead of hers, even though I was too young to have a memory. When she told it to other people, she never ended at the part I would have, the part where we survived the car accident. Where we walked away without a scratch. She always went on to talk about the time her foot got caught in train tracks, how she struggled to get free, and how if it had happened five seconds later, she would have died. And the fire in her apartment building two years before she met my dad—*oh, did you hear about it?* Everyone had heard about it. Six people dead, including her neighbors on both sides, and it happened ten minutes after she left for work one morning.

She talked about the chest infection I got when I was two. I was in the hospital for days, and I should have died.

When I was little and fell and scraped my knee, my mother would always whisper the same thing in my ear. Other mothers said, "Shh, it's okay," and coaxed the tears away with a soft-serve cone. Mine said, "Come on, Danielle. You're the girl with nine lives. You take after me."

I don't think she ever whispered that in Jena's ear. That's the difference.

I always pretended to believe her just so she would leave me alone, but I knew my mother was full of crap. I *knew* not to take her seriously. Her words floated above my ears, leaped out of windows and into trees, were carried away by birds and dusty-winged moths and other things I knew to be true.

Then Jena happened.

Nothing and everything is true. We are papier-mâché in a world with a cardboard sun. There is no such thing as cold or heat or time. We are all the same people, constantly being re-born and redying, and every time we think it's the first.

A month ago, we found out Jena's treatment isn't working like they'd hoped and that she needs bone marrow. We thought I'd be the one to help her. I have marrow and plenty of bone and I am her twin.

But we are too different and the doctors can't break me into splintered little fragments to save Jena. Mom and Dad aren't a match either, but I am her twin.

Everything Mom had ever said crept back in under the door of my room, tucked itself in my ears when I was sleeping. I hid it under the pillows and breathed it in at night. I couldn't fall asleep either. And I can't forget.

Am I the girl with nine lives?

I wish I could forget.

One of the times Mom told her story—about when we'd survived, our nine lives—my Uncle Stephan was visiting. He was some college professor that was a friend of my dad's, one of those people you call "uncle" without ever knowing why, without them earning the title. Abandoning his standard topic of conspiracy theories for a while, he started talking about all the explanations for the nine lives myth. He said that every time a cat loses one of its lives, that life is released into the universe, to be caught by another cat. Not all cats are born with nine lives, but those that aren't can keep as many as they can catch. One extra life, or two, or three.

As one life shortens, the other expands.

Now my mother tries to stay awake, while I try to fall asleep.

My eyelids finally collapse on themselves just as the sun feels it's safe to come out of hiding. It's less than two hours before school starts, but that's the way it always goes.

The next thing I know, Mom is shaking me awake and

joking about how much I like my beauty sleep. I play along, turning over and waiting until the last possible minute to get up and go.

By the time I shower and get downstairs, the only other person I've seen today is Mom. Dad's already at work.

"Morning, Danielle." I jump when I hear Jena's voice from the top of the stairs. I always aim to be out of the house before she's awake.

"Hey," I say. She's leaning against the railing, looking down at me.

I've never understood why anyone would mix Jena and me up. We are fraternal twins, and since elementary school, I've been about an inch taller. My hair is long, brunette, and straight, while hers was wavy, sort of a mousy brown.

"I'm late for the bus."

She frowns, because she knows I'm not, but I've already grabbed my backpack, deciding against breakfast, and am heading toward the front door.

It is bright out, but cold. Dirty, weeks-old snow is slathered unevenly over the ground like a moldy spread on an open-face sandwich.

When the bus finally pulls up at the stop down the street from my house, I drag my way to the back, placing my backpack in the seat beside me, and pressing my face against the window, eyes shut, until we get to school.

2

The best thing about weekday mornings is math class. Really. Our teacher, Mr. Halbrook, was a political science minor in college and hasn't forgotten it. We're more likely to discuss foreign policy than algebra in this class. Which goes over about as well as you'd imagine with tenth graders as well versed in the art of apathy as we are.

"Hey, Dani," my friend Lauren says as I enter the room, just before the bell goes off. I'm heading toward my usual seat behind her when I note that there's an even better one across the aisle from her.

"Lauren, hope you don't mind if I sit here today," I tell her, grinning. She tucks a black braid behind her ear and rolls her eyes in response.

I shift closer to Jack Penner, the guy in the seat on the other side of mine. "How's it going, hot stuff?"

Jack glances up from his book temporarily, a healthy flush coloring his cheeks. Poor kid. Some people would call what

I do to Jack bullying, but you have to understand that I've known him since elementary school. We have a connection.

I squeeze his shoulder and turn to Lauren.

"So I'm putting up Green Society posters today in fifth period, if you want to come help," she says as Mr. Halbrook walks in, hugging a pregnant yellow folder. "Crap. I hope those aren't our tests."

"I have gym," I say regretfully. "Maybe I'll just tell Mr. K. I have excruciating cramps and have to skip."

Lauren makes a face. "I hate girls who use cramps as an excuse to get out of stuff."

I don't react to Lauren's insult because she's genuinely oblivious to the fact that she's just insulted me. Her motto is to speak her mind always. It's why I'm her only real friend and why she's the only friend I've kept.

"I think it's the ultimate slap in the face of feminism," she continues as Mr. Halbrook drops her marked test in front of her.

"Great job," he nods. She looks down at her paper and beams.

"Wow, I didn't do that badly." Which means she could only have gotten a hundred percent.

While she's looking over her test, I turn to Jack. "Hey, Jack, can I ask you something? What's another word for cramps? I think *that* word is a slap in the face of humanism."

The tips of Jack's ears redden.

"Uh, I don't know," he stutters. Jack is an overachieving

nerd with zero social skills. Always has been. He has also always been lanky, with bluish-gray eyes and blond hair.

I prop my face up in my hand and continue. "I'm sure it has a synonym. It's like the word 'diarrhea.'"

As luck would have it, Mr. Halbrook just happens to be dropping off my test, and he shoots me a disapproving look. I'm not sure if it's because of my test score or the conversation I'm having. Probably both.

I give him a winning smile and tuck my test into the back of my notebook without looking at it. "Everybody calls it 'diarrhea' or 'the runs,' which are equally as bad as each other and the condition that they describe. Don't you think?"

Jack keeps his head down, staring intently at his notebook. A test paper with a circled green 98 lands in front of him.

"Wow, good job," I say.

"Thanks."

"Anyway," I continue, doodling on the inside cover of my notebook. "Whoever came up with those words deserves to be shot. But it turns out another synonym for diarrhea is 'Montezuma's revenge,' which is a thousand times better. And actually makes me *wish* I had it."

A few people are eavesdropping on our conversation now, and I hear them snicker. Jack is still ignoring me. Lauren is fascinated with her test. I wonder how she stands it, being perfect. There's nothing to feel guilty or angry about, nothing to improve or argue over.

"So I was just kind of wondering if it's the same thing with cramps. Maybe it can be, like, the Serpent's Revenge or God's Revenge or something."

"Like the Garden of Eden." Jack looks as surprised as I feel that he spoke up.

I nudge him with my shoulder. "*Somebody* listened in Sunday school."

He goes back to ignoring me. Presumably Jack Penner doesn't enjoy being patronized.

"How did you do?" Lauren whispers, as Mr. Halbrook announces that we'll be "exploring the relationship between the economy and math." At least he's making the effort to relate them today.

"Not very well," I answer even though I haven't actually looked at it. But looking is overrated, a waste of time.

"You know," she whispers back, "with a little effort, I bet you could be smart again."

I give her a grateful smile but don't say anything.

3

Before I was This, I used to eat lunch with Lauren, Holly, and Renee. Preppy, clean-cut girls who cared about academics (Lauren), Jesus (Holly), and boys (Renee). My parents couldn't have been prouder.

I cared that I had somewhere to sit at lunch, a safe and predictable haven, where we were all girls that were generally well-liked (Lauren didn't count), had never been to a funeral (Holly didn't count), and were destined to remain virgins till at least college (Renee didn't count).

Occasionally I still eat with Lauren, but Holly and Renee never know what to do around me anymore, and it's easier for all of us to avoid each other.

So I tend to float around these days, sharing my company with only the most deserving.

Today, I sit at the far end of the cafeteria in the spot usually reserved for the deadbeats/Goths, warily unwrapping the tofu sandwich Mom left on the counter for me this morning, when I hear a sigh followed by a tray slamming hard against the table.

"Great. You again."

I glance up to see Candy Jansen and, I swear, my heart constricts a little for her. The girl is a whole different breed of Goth. But with a name like Candy, she was never going to make it anyway.

I beam at her. "Spencer invited me to eat with you guys any time I want."

"Well, *Spencer* will probably be a while. The lunch line is super long."

I stifle a laugh. "Is that mascara running down your face?" She looks like she's been through a coal mine. Even gym class couldn't do that to a person.

Candy narrows her eyes so they disappear completely. "Ha. Ha. Is that 'Not Funny' tattooed on your forehead?" She sits across from me.

I'm really not in the mood to exchange insults with Candy, but I don't have anything better to do—plus tofu makes me barf—so I quip, "It's possible. But I don't know how you'd be able to tell with those caterpillar eyelashes. New look?"

Her nostrils flare as she tears open a packet of ketchup. "Bitch," she hisses as Spencer puts his tray next to mine and sits down.

With a condescending smile, I whisper, "Tryhard," which, by my standards, is infinitely worse. "Hey, Spencer," I say. Two guys—one of whom I recognize from the bus—plop into seats beside him, and quickly become embroiled in some game on Electric Blue Mane's laptop.

I assume Spencer can hear the claws retracting, because he's smiling and shaking his head at me and Candy. As far as hardcore teenagers go, Spencer Lloyd is the real deal. With more tattoos than I can count all over his body, a smoke-spewing Harley, and a newly shaved head, he's Quentin High's resident bad boy. I've even heard rumors about juvie.

Then, there's Candy. Candy's jet-black hair, runny mascara, and ripped jeans are as translucently poserish as you can get. Up until a year ago, her locker was adorned with dog-eared horse posters. Like me, she hopes some of Spencer will rub off on her and make people take her more seriously. It's probably why I hate her so much. I never like people like me.

"Spencer," Candy whines, "don't you feel like this whole damn town is dead? It's so, like, quiet and *cold*."

I take a sip of my juice. "Well, it *is* February. Don't quote me on this, but I heard winter is typically the coldest time of year."

Candy sends me a look that tells me she wasn't talking to me and wouldn't mind if I fell off the face of the Earth.

"There's a party this weekend," Spencer answers.

"Perfect." Candy claps her hands. "When and where?"

"Seven on Saturday. My cousin's place on the west side. I'll text it to you later."

I stare at my sandwich and contemplate taking a bite. Candy says something about being thirsty. I think she's hoping Spencer will offer her some of his chocolate milk, but he doesn't. I wonder if she pisses him off as much as she does me.

Candy stands and sighs. "I guess I'll just go get myself a

drink." Spencer's only response comes in the form of a slurp, and so she sulks off. My eyes wander across the cafeteria, taking in all the cliques. The dancers. The cheerleaders. The preps—my old friends. The jocks. Jena could have sat anywhere, but she usually sat over there with them. Lindsay, Khy, and Erin are laughing at something Ben Hershey is saying. There's no sign that Jena ever went to school here, had friends and a lunch table, or went to Spring Fling with Ben last year.

"I'm guessing you have plans for Saturday," Spencer whispers close to my ear. The hairs in my ear and on the back of my neck tickle, and I turn to face him. "With your busy schedule and everything."

"Yeah. I'll probably be trying to find a real party."

He laughs. "Trust me, nobody does parties like Nelson."

"Mandela?"

He shakes his head and goes back to eating.

Candy returns, bearing gifts. "Spence, I brought you another drink." She slides a carton across to him. Evidently, where she comes from, flavored milk is the way to a man's heart. Candy spends the rest of lunchtime flirting with him, which is fine because I'm not listening anyway.

As the bell rings, signaling the end of lunch, Spencer says, "Dani, you should at least check it out. Text me if you want the address."

"We'll see."

He winks at me before turning to go. "I'll keep an eye out for you."

I wish all days were extinct, but as of today, Wednesday tops my list.

Jena is in the second week of a two-week block of radiation treatments. Wednesdays are Jena's "long" days, which just means her appointment starts and ends later. Before radiation, Jena used to spend weeks at a time in the hospital getting chemo. So, really, this new arrangement—chemo pills and one block of radiation—where she gets to come home every day, is like winning the cancer treatment lottery.

But this Wednesday afternoon finds me sitting on a cold hospital room floor pretending to do homework, as far from my sister's bed as I can get without being absent altogether.

Mom had me take the bus here after school today, because my dad is taking me to an audition this afternoon and picking me up from the hospital, which is closer to his work than home would be. My mother also thought it would be good for me and Jena to "spend some time together." But, as I sit here, I can't help straining my ears and counting the number of times Jena breathes in and out. *In* and *out*. Maybe, if I listen hard enough, I'll hear a secret code, a message that will prepare me for whatever comes next, but there's only the whirring of machines and her inhaling and exhaling.

Mom has been gone for nearly half an hour. I imagine she's off somewhere prodding Jena's doctors and trying to force good news out of them.

I hear the shuffle of sneakers coming down the hall, followed by the rolling wheels of the cart he delivers pitchers of water on. And by "he," I mean Rufus, the volunteer boy my sister is in love with. Rufus is seventeen, with shaggy brown hair that always needs a trim. He isn't bad-looking, and I'm learning to look past the name, even though I will always consider Rufus to be a dog's name. Wednesdays just happen to be his volunteer days.

Today, when he stops by her room, Jena puts her book down and says, "Are you, like, obsessed with water? I never see you without fifteen gallons of it." Sadly, this is my sister's best attempt at flirtation.

Instead of hightailing it out of here, Rufus laughs and injects a lame barb of his own.

I realize it must mean he's in love with her, too. Oh, there have been signs all along. The way he used to call her "Viva La Jenavieva" until Jena told him to *seriously, stop*. That time he lent her one of his most-cherished Alice Cooper CDs. *Of course.* He has a thing for pasty sixteen-year-old girls in hospital beds. Why has it taken so long for me to figure this out?

They flirt—if you can call it that—for a couple of minutes before Rufus leaves. Jena goes back to reading, and the room goes back to being silent. But silence is the sound of her breathing and I can't stand the way it pokes at my ribs and makes it hard for me to breathe, too. Especially when I'm already being manhandled by chem homework I can't do. I also know that Jena isn't really reading—only pretending to—and I want to fill her head with something else, something other than what the doctors might be telling Mom right now.

So I tell Jena about Rufus being in love with her. She tries to act dismissive, but I see her eyes light up just a little and I can't hear her breathing, which is good. Then somehow I am ducking out of her room and chasing Rufus down the hall, while Jena calls me back and yells, "I'm never, ever going to forgive you if you say anything to him!"

I spot him near the end of the hallway, his cart rickety as he gets ready to turn the corner. And then, suddenly, he stops. When he turns to face me, we stare at each other for an awkward moment. Maybe two.

Then I stick out my hand. "I'm Dani, Jena's sister."

"Yeah, I know . . ." He looks at me, waiting. Right now, I should be noticing how Rufus's hair hangs over the collar of his shirt, and the fact that it looks a little greasy up close. It should occur to me that Jena can do better. A lot better.

Instead, I am thinking about the fact that I just said I was Jena's sister and that might not always be true. I am thinking of other things I could be instead—my mother's daughter, my friend's friend, my body's inhabitant—and I can't think of a single one that sounds okay. "Maybe you and Jena could go on a date sometime. She'd really like that," I say.

His eyes do a weird little dance. Rounder—no, narrower—no. Scared?

He looks back at his cart. "I . . . Yeah, maybe," and I can tell he is lying, and if he does think about it, she'll just be the sick girl that flirts with him when he delivers water and I'll just be her weird sister.

"Maybe?" I repeat, raising an eyebrow.

"Maybe," he says again, and then pushes his cart around the corner before I can say anything else.

I stand there for a moment, hoping Mom will come so I won't have to go back and tell Jena. Eventually, I drag my feet toward her room. Why did I ever think convincing her that a boy-who-wasn't-good-enough-for-her liked her was better than hearing her breathe?

This is why it's easier not to say anything to Jena. I always say the wrong thing. Now I am afraid she is going to cry.

But as soon as I walk into her room, she snaps her book shut, blinks away the hope in her eyes, and smirks. "Let me guess. He thinks I'm contagious?"

I bite the inside of my cheek. I want to tell her it's because he hasn't seen her play soccer or heard her laugh yet—her *real* laugh, not the one she reserves for hospitals. It isn't breathy or forced or hard to listen to.

She shakes her head, smiles. "God. What a tool." I want

to remember this—the moment when, even though I'd been a complete fool, she wasn't crying, she wasn't breathing too loud, and I was still Jena's sister. I am still Jena's sister.

I sit back down in my corner right below the window of her room, both of us ignoring the fact that she is secretly disappointed.

"And I can't *believe*," she says, "you tried to set me up with someone named Rufus. I hate you."

And suddenly she is laughing, a loud, full sound that takes up the whole room, makes it feel like she's right beside me. I want to bottle it up and save it for next time. I'll play it over one of her hospital laughs, over the sound of her fighting to breathe.

Forty minutes later, while Jena is fast asleep, Mom walks in and says Dad is waiting for me outside the hospital.

She watches me, imparting all manner of "helpful" tips, while I close up my books and stuff them into my backpack. Mom's particularly excited about this audition because the commercial is being directed by a former actor she used to work with, a Brody Richardson.

"He's really a fan of the postmodern, so subtlety is key," Mom says right before I head outside. I have no idea what she is talking about and leave her sitting in the chair beside Jena, flipping through one of the medical journals she subscribes to.

Three minutes later, I'm at the east entrance to the hospital atrium, and so is Dad.

We pull out of the parking lot and get on the highway from Quentin to Robindale. Now, all of a sudden, Dad looks worried. This is his first time taking me to an audition. "Are you ready? You don't need your lines or makeup or something?"

In lieu of an answer, I say, "So, you're just blowing off work to take me to some audition?"

"Now," Dad says, "it's not just *some audition*. You know how much this means to your mother. Besides, I've arranged for my work schedule to be a little more flexible for the next few months. To accommodate."

My mother is determined to make sure that nothing else changes, but, in doing so, she's implementing all sorts of changes. My father leaving work early? Taking me to auditions?

"Personally," I say, "I think we should put the whole acting thing on the back burner for now." For now. To accommodate. We speak in half-finished sentences because we're terrified to know how they truly end. Maybe it's not for now, but for ever. Maybe it's not until. Or maybe it is.

Dad glances at me and pats my knee. "There's no reason for that." He does a shoulder check and changes lanes. "Actually, I'm glad we have some time to talk."

I don't want to know how this part ends either, so I lean against the window, duck my head, and pretend to sleep. Somewhere between Quentin and Robindale, it becomes real and I'm floating above myself, the car, everything, fast asleep, as my father's voice reappears in interludes.

At some point, I'm not sure when, he realizes I'm asleep and turns on the radio to drown out the silence.

He alternates between singing and tapping along to James Brown. There's a very good reason why we have a no-singing-along rule implemented for all family road trips, and this is it.

I swear, I consider waking up and having that father-daughter conversation just to make him stop.

Maybe I'm not asleep after all.

5

Dad and I are sitting in a conference room at Robindale's Ramada, where the audition is being held, and the room is bleeding maroon. Loose purple-red fibers dangle from the curtain, like trickles from bursting capillaries. The worn burgundy carpet seems to be past its expiration date.

There are twenty of us in total—eleven parents, nine kids. Dozens of covert glances are shot across the room, everyone trying to hide the fact that they're sizing up the competition.

So far, no sign of Brody Richardson.

"What do we do now?" Dad asks.

"Well." I lean back in my chair, the piece of paper the receptionist gave me rustling in my lap. "This is usually the part where Mom flirts with the casting director or the occasional stage dad."

My father's eyes widen.

I pat his shoulder. "It's only your first day. It's not like I expect you to jump right into Mom's role. Baby steps, okay?"

"Very funny," he says with a shake of his head. I go back to eyeballing the other kids here, each of them accompanied by a version of my mother—a parent whose own hopes of superstardom rest squarely on the shoulders of her wimpy child.

My father's too oblivious to be pushy.

I've never quite figured out how to play the whole acting thing. I've been in school plays and had a role in Quentin Community Theatre's production of *Oklahoma!* two years ago. It was only about a year ago that Mom had me start trying out for commercials. The truth is, I can tolerate acting just enough to keep doing auditions and make my mother happy, and I dislike it just enough to maintain my street cred. But it's also a distraction, for me and for my parents. Which is simultaneously good and bad.

Mom always went with me to auditions, partly because she wanted to make sure I did it right and partly because we had an unspoken understanding that this was more about her than me.

"I was trying to talk to you in the car, before you fell asleep," Dad says now.

"Oh, right. Yeah. I do that a lot, actually. I'm starting to think I have narcolepsy."

Dad doesn't react. "I wanted to talk to you about . . . Jena. And how you're dealing with the situation."

He leaves some dot-dot-dots for me to fill in, but continues when my lips don't part. "This is hard on all of us. Your mother and I are worried about the toll it's taken on you. The last thing we want is for you to feel left out or like you're taking a backseat to your sister."

I let out a small laugh. "Trust me, I don't feel that way at all." And I really don't. If this were a movie, maybe I would. I'd be the kid that gets shipped from extended family member to extended family member, tanking at school, seeking attention, a lost little girl. Instead, I'm sitting at an audition for a toothpaste commercial with my father. If my mother had her way, she'd be here instead. In a heartbeat, she'd be here. But we can't always have what we want. So no, I'm not feeling left out.

"Well, I'm glad," Dad says with a smile. *I'm* glad to be able to make him feel a little less guilty. Everybody needs that once in a while. "You know that if you ever need anything, even if it's something small—it doesn't even matter—your mother and I are never too busy. You and Jena are the most precious things in the world to us." *Precious stones.* "Precious stones."

"I know."

"Good."

My father calls Jena and me his "precious stones" because we went through this phase in second grade when we were weirdly fascinated by rocks. At the time, Dad thought it would be cute and very Mike Brady to point out that we loved our stones, but he loved *us* more than we loved them. We were *his* special stones. Precious stones.

While Dad flips open a newspaper, I say, "I'll keep an eye out for hot stage parents. I assume you prefer moms?"

He chuckles, shakes his head, and starts reading.

I lean back in my chair and stare up at the light blue ceiling. There's a window right above our seats, and sunshine streams through it.

Just then someone sits with a thud in the chair beside me. A tall redhead with a regrettable perm and a blue dress much too fancy for this place. She rests her head against the wall and sniffs, and I note that her eyes are red, angry, and liquid.

The girl's mother sits down beside her, and begins to do what one can only describe as hissing. Pageant Girl tries to argue back, but clearly the taps behind her eyes are broken and they rush open and spill all over her face. Everyone in the room stares at them, and some people whisper. In fact, the only person who doesn't seem to notice is her mother.

This scene with Pageant Girl and her mother reminds me of the time Jena dyed her hair blond in seventh grade, the day after I got the part of Glinda in the school play. Her hair turned out awful. She called me from the top of the stairs, her voice shaky and horrified and scared. There wasn't much we could do but go to Mom. And Mom yelled for hours, cried, and called Aunt Tish to ask where'd she gone wrong as a mother, *please God can somebody tell me.* The thing is, Mom should have been grateful. She should have wrapped Jena up in her long, Pilates-did-this arms and squeezed her. Jena could easily have dyed her hair lime or orange. Lime and orange were blatant, glow-in-the-dark acts of rebellion, guaranteed to bring Mom weeks of public humiliation, and they'd probably have suited Jena better. Going blond wasn't a ploy to hurt Mom; it was the closest Jena ever came to doing something so Mom would see her.

I snap back to reality, and my ears ring from all the not-quite-yelling.

"Unacceptable ought to be ashamed foolish irresponsible Andrea angry disappointed whatyoudid unacceptable ought to be ashamed . . . Andrea," Pageant Girl's mother whispers, only occasionally stopping for breaths.

During one of those breaks, against my better judgment, I turn toward Andrea and speak. "Is your mom married?"

She looks at me for a second, like she can't quite understand me, and her mother's head has snapped in my direction now, too.

Andrea wipes her wet cheek with the back of her hand and shakes her head.

"Dad," I stage-whisper, and give him a nudge. A did-you-hear-*that* nudge.

This time it's his head that snaps up. "What?"

"*You know,*" I say, nudging him again as Andrea, her mom, and the whole room look on. So much for inconspicuous nudging.

My father's face flushes and he mutters, "Cut it out, Dani."

Except, maybe Andrea's mom hears him, too, because she also cuts it out. And we can all sit in peace. You'd think someone planned it.

Andrea owes my father a snazzy thank-you note. She might also want to consider dyeing her hair something glow-in-the-dark, to fix her mom issues. Or getting cancer.

Dad folds his arms across his chest and sits there, embarrassed, until someone comes to take me to the other conference room across the hall, so I can repeat lines about how this brand of toothpaste has changed my life.

Dad is allowed to come in and watch me. He stands at the back and gives me a thumbs-up, but by the fourth time they've made me repeat the lines, he is looking around the room, taking in the cameras and all the bigwigs that sell toothpaste and plastic smiles for a living. When he asks, they tell him that Brody Richardson is finishing up an off-Broadway producing gig and will be here for later rounds. I'm not sure whether Mom will be impressed, or disappointed he's not here.

After it's over and after their promise of "we'll be in touch," we leave. Dad is so pleased with both of us that he pulls into a McDonald's drive-through, and asks me to pick anything I want. Apparently, he has not noticed that we've eaten nothing but tofu and organic food for the past seven months. But I don't say anything. I order a double Big Mac, and we make a big show of acting like everything is the way it always was. Until we have to go home, and we can't pretend anymore.

6

The best thing about my parents right now is how willing they are to overcompensate.

"Lauren's here!" I jump up and button my sweater.

They also trust me, which helps.

"When does this movie marathon finish? Are you sure you don't want me to come and pick you up from the theater?"

"Dad, please," I groan, heading toward the front door. He stops me to plant a kiss on my forehead and I yell goodbye to Mom in the kitchen. "Where's Jena?" I ask.

"Resting," he answers. "She's had a rough day." Mom's spent the whole day at attention because Jena has been running a fever, and if it gets up to 102, they have to go to the emergency room.

I think he's waiting for me to go upstairs and say goodbye, but I know my sister would be totally onto me. Plus, I might talk myself out of going if I have to see her. "Tell her I say bye."

I hurry out the front door and get into Lauren's car. She

and her sister are going to the cineplex in the mall. I'm going to Spencer's cousin's party.

"Thanks for the ride," I tell her as I slip in. Her older sister, Nicole, sits in the front seat beside her and gives me a tight smile. She's a Ph.D. candidate in sociology and I can tell she doesn't approve of sixteen-year-olds who lie to their parents and wear pink cardigans and sensible jeans to parties.

"No problem. Do you want us to pick you up after the movies?"

"Nah. If I can't bum a ride at an overcrowded party, I've failed."

"You know, I still think you should come with us. Apart from being entertaining, the Indiana Jones films are also highly educational." Only Lauren would consider that a good thing. "And Harrison Ford is so handsome," she continues, grinning at her sister. "He's Nicole's favorite."

I sigh. "See, I've never really grasped his appeal. Probably because he looks a little like my grandpa."

A sudden silence descends over us. Was it something I said?

I see Nicole square her shoulders, then she turns up the radio and Celine Dion streams out from the speakers. The speakers in the back are so loud, they crackle when Celine reaches her glory notes, and my seat vibrates.

Soon, we've reached our destination. A suburban house on a dark street with scores of people streaming in and out of it.

"Dani, I feel bad leaving you here all by yourself. Even

though I can't understand why you'd come to a party like this, I don't want you to wind up dead or something."

"You're too sweet, Lauren," I tell her as I take off my seatbelt. "But all I can ask is that you get ready to be my phone-a-friend if this place gets busted."

Nicole throws me a look I can only describe as disgusted. I'm willing to bet she'll be telling her younger sister to stay the hell away from me from now on, before the car door has even shut on Celine's musical declaration of longing.

After worming my way inside the house, the first person I recognize is Candy.

I hope it's not a sign of how my evening is going to go.

She's leaning against a wall, talking to a couple of people I don't know. I should walk right by her and pretend not to see her, but I stop.

"Hey, have you seen Spencer?" I ask.

"No." She brushes a sticky strand of hair from her face with her thumb. "But he said he'd come and find me as soon as he got here. So I guess he's not here yet."

I pull out my cell phone and check the time. 8:28. Somehow I don't see Spencer missing over an hour of a party. "You're right. He's probably behind on homework. You know how he likes to stay on top of things," I tell Candy, and quite possibly she believes me.

Even Spencer's fashionably absent parents know the last piece of homework he handed in was in eighth grade. But Candy's always been a little slow on the uptake.

"Well, tell him I'm looking for him, if you see him."

"Okay," she lies.

I turn and elbow my way through the swarms of people.

I need to find something to drink and Spencer. In that order.

While I'm in the kitchen getting a drink, I run into the last person I ever expected to meet at a crazy house party.

"Well, hello, sexy thang," I say, adopting a sober slur. Somehow they're not as fun as drunken ones. Bringing the plastic cup to my lips, I smile at Jack Penner. "Fancy seeing you here."

His eyes scamper across the room, and he looks a tad claustrophobic. Almost as claustrophobic as I feel.

I put one arm on the cold kitchen countertop. "Hope I didn't keep you waiting too long."

"I'm, uh, actually here with someone else." He glances over his shoulder as if hoping for the person to suddenly materialize.

"Is there a rule saying you can only talk to the person you came with?"

"Actually, um, it's just Sandeep. Nelson's his lab partner, and he invited him, but Sandeep was too scared to come alone and convinced R.J. and Toby and me to come with, so . . ." Jack's explanation fades with a gulp.

"Sounds . . . kinky?" I say.

The light in here affects everything with a yellow tinge, but I think it's safe to say that Jack is blushing. Suddenly I'm bored. I stand up straighter. "Well, have fun tonight."

I turn and leave him, beginning what amounts to a night of searching for more drinks and Spencer—again, in that order—and bumping into Candy, who tries entirely too hard to make it look like she's having a wonderful time. Every time I see her, she's thrusting her chin in the air, laughing like everything is So Damn Funny.

I run into Renee Garcia, of people-I-used-to-eat-lunch-with fame, and her boyfriend, a senior with ears that stick out and a five o'clock shadow. I'm not expecting her to slide closer to him so I have a place to sit, but she does. I hesitate, but finally sit. The room is no longer as steady as it once was, and the people in the corners of the room look fuzzy.

Renee asks how I've been and how Jena is.

I copy and paste two "fines," and then, halfway through her introducing me to her new boyfriend, she slinks even closer to him and starts digging her fingers through the spikes in his hair. I take that as my cue to leave and let them be alone with the fifty-seven other people in this room.

"As per my predictions," I tell Spencer, when I finally run into him sometime around ten and after I've had way more success finding drinks, "this party sucks."

"Well, it doesn't look like you've had *too* much of a bad time," he remarks, noting the cup in my hand and the way I can't exactly stand up straight.

We are side by side, both of us facing forward and unwisely leaning back on a cabinet that features expensive little glass ornaments from all of Nelson's parents' exotic upper-middle-class vacations.

"What can we do to accommodate your impossibly high

party standards?" Spencer has his arms folded across his chest, watching me from the corner of his eye, and I wonder where he has been. What exactly do non-posers do at parties? He doesn't even seem wasted. Suddenly he lets out a small laugh. "You know people are still talking about that party in September? You're kind of a legend."

I give a small smile.

At a party thrown by I-don't-know-who, I got dared to eat this concoction some kids had mixed together. It contained mustard, raw eggs, soymilk, and sesame seeds, but those were just the ingredients I could recognize when they were coming back out. The beers I'd flown through that night probably didn't help, either.

It was nearly two months after Jena got sick, the first big party after school started, when all I wanted was to be someone else, to not be the sick girl's twin sister. I was hacking in the bushes in front of I-don't-know-who's house, post-concoction, when I finally realized I couldn't be anyone else. I didn't deserve to be anyone else, to be at a party or even at school, not while Jena was elsewhere dissolving.

"That was fun," Spencer muses.

"It was okay."

He shifts even closer to me now so our hands are almost touching on the cabinet, but still doesn't face me. "Well, as I said, tell me what I can do to accommodate your needs and I'll do my best."

Just then, some guy comes up to Spencer and starts talking

his ear off. Spencer tells me he'll be right back and they walk away, leaving me still leaning against the cabinet, alone.

It's only after he's gone that I realize that Spencer might have meant something I hadn't even considered. It's weird to think about. He's cute, but . . .

The last hour is a bit of a blur. I only know that Spencer doesn't come back. I think for a second that I see Candy, but she's curled up on a couch by herself, crying, so that can't be right.

I drink some more. I stumble outside.

It's freezing and I'm underdressed. I sit down on a step at the back of the house and press my palm against the wall. The house is convulsing, shaking, not like it wants to collapse, but as if it wants to expel all the people inside it. I keep my hand flat on the wall, with my ear close to it so I can hear it screaming.

Too many people. Must get them out. And, *Are you scared?*

"No, I'm not scared," I whisper back. "Are you?"

I'm waiting for its reply when I hear feet crunching against the snow, moving toward me.

"Are you talking to yourself?" Pause. "Or the building?"

The person sounds so far away, standing up while I'm crouched down with my face still up against the wall.

"No, I'm not scared. Who are you?"

It's all a blur, but somehow I get home. Maybe it's a Good Samaritan. Renee or some other person I know peripherally from school. Probably it's Spencer.

It doesn't even matter, but I'm so wasted, I keep imagining it's Jack Penner.

7

The world is fast asleep. Or, at least, the one within these four corners. I stumble to the kitchen, find a glass, and gulp down two cups of water. Then I make my way upstairs, careful to pick up the various items I knock down. I tiptoe down the hall and instead of going right, I go wrong.

Stuck on Jena's door is a newspaper cutout from when her soccer team won state almost two years ago. There's a black-and-white picture of the entire team: messy ponytails, grassy white uniforms, and glistening smiles. Next to it is a piece of paper with a picture of a skull and a No Entry sign that has been up there even longer. The papers rustle, jeering at me as I barge into Jena's room without knocking, momentarily fearing an impassioned tirade about boundaries and *respect*. But this Jena is as weak as the pieces of paper on her door that are missing corners; there is no tirade.

I close the door partway before I head to her bed. Fortunately, there is nothing to trip over in here. My parents are in and out so often that they've adjusted the room to suit their needs.

I find her buried under a pile of blankets. Peel off the first layer and she's not there. Peel off the second, the third, the fourth. There's Jena Baby. That's where she's hiding.

"Jena," I whisper close to her ear. "Jena, wake up."

She moans and pulls the last blanket back over her.

"Jena." I shake her gently. "Wake up. I want to show you something."

A couple of minutes later, she finally opens her eyes. The darkness swallows her pupils and mostly I see the white in her eyes. "What's going on?"

"Shh."

She sits up slowly. "You stink. Are you drunk?"

"Will you please come outside with me? I want to show you something."

Jena appraises me for a second. "Right now?" I hang my head. "I'm really tired, Dani."

"It won't take long, I promise."

It's almost midnight. We have two hours before Mom is up and about.

"Fine."

I watch as she gets out of bed, gently, like she's afraid she'll break something. I stand back and stare, not sure whether to offer my services or let her be.

She tells me where her coat is and I help her put it on. My fingers accidentally jab at her waist, or maybe it's not her waist, and I pause.

"Here." I untangle two other blankets from the pile and

make her stand still while I Saran-Wrap her in them. Around and around so she doesn't break on the way down the stairs. "One more." So the cold doesn't get into her chest.

"Let's go."

I help her downstairs and we head out the back door. Outside, it still looks like night. Somebody needs to do something about the way time works around here, push it back some. Midnight is too early to be a new day.

"What is it?" Jena asks, her teeth chattering. I look away from her, annoyed at how her teeth clash and run into each other, how her lips are a tinge of moonlight blue even though we've only been out a minute. It's not even that cold.

I don't say anything, just point up at the sky. The stars look like smudged glitter on a messy kindergarten project.

The snow on the ground is dry, almost hard, compared to fresh snow. But as I walk, the ice crust on the top layer breaks under my shoes. Jena follows me further into the yard, but stops when I'm in a pile of snow up to my ankles. I sit first and then lie down in my bed of snow. Jena just looks at me and, for a second, I'm certain she's going to turn around and go back into the house.

A moment later, though, she's sitting down on a slightly shallower patch. Neither of us speaks and I listen for the sound of squirrels or owls or Mrs. Frisby and the other rats from that book Dad used to read to us when we were little. I bet there's a snake out here tonight. A winter snake.

Didn't I use to be afraid of these things?

"Once upon a time," her voice cuts into the darkness, "there was an elf named Billy."

There's a silence, signaling my turn.

"Billy was deathly allergic to tomatoes. They made him sneeze."

Once upon a time, Jena and I used to make up fairy tales. We'd be driving to visit our grandparents in Michigan, or heading to the mall or a dentist's appointment. The only rule was that there were to be no princesses (they were so overdone, Jena said) and no fairy godmothers (too much of a cop-out), and no dragons. The no-dragon thing was my contribution. I have something against dragons, and I don't mind that they all seem to be extinct.

Everything else, though, is fair game.

"Every time Billy came near a tomato, he started wheezing. He'd say, 'Get that to . . . to . . . tom-AH-to away from me,'" Jena says. "And that's where the big argument comes from. Tomato, tom-ah-to. Anyway, one day, as Billy was walking home from elf school, he ran into a wizard."

"The wizard's name was Harry," I start, only to be instantly interrupted by Jena.

"His name can't be Harry. That's lame."

I sit up. "Excuse me, did I interrupt your story? And, if you remember, there are no rules, Jenavieve."

I don't mind if you call me Danielle. I don't even mind if you call *me* Jenavieve, but don't call my sister that.

Her knuckles make contact with my shoulder before she

takes over. "The wizard's name was Alfonso, and he'd spent his entire life searching for Billy." Her teeth are like cymbals clanging against each other. Three blankets is not enough, but three blankets swallows her whole. Look at her eyes. Jena Baby needs one more layer. Or three. "You see, it turns out that although Billy had been born an elf, on his seventh birthday—"

A door suddenly slams and a cold wind travels toward us, bringing with it my mother. "Oh my God," she yells, "are you crazy?" A rhetorical question. She picks Jena up off the ground, removing the robe she's flung over her pajamas and trying to slip it on over my sister's cocoon. I was right that she needed one more blanket. "Do you know how cold it is out here? What were you thinking?"

She hustles Jena inside, depositing a few teaspoons of saliva on her face, I'm sure, because while she's mostly yelling at me, she's too distraught to turn her back on my sister.

"Mom, it's okay," Jena protests, but her arguments fall on deaf ears.

I trail behind them until they disappear into the house, and then I turn around and go back to where we were sitting.

We never got to finish our story, but it's better that way. The best ones aren't supposed to end. My mother is still inside tending to Jena and tucking her blankets underneath her mattress, so they don't slip out and let her fall. But even though she's not here this instant, I know what Mom wants to say to me, what she's thinking right now.

Are you insane, Danielle? Did you bring her out here to die? How many times do I have to tell you that she's not like us?

And she's right. What was I thinking? Jena has a fever, and those things matter now. Everything matters.

The air feels thick, chilly, the same way it suddenly did that night when I saw the bruises, even though that was summer and this is winter. It was some nighttime barbecue in July, and I think I was standing right here and Jena was standing right there. They were blue and gray, just under her shoulder blades. A blue and gray that would have looked beautiful in the sky, but not on my sister's back. Blue and grays aren't supposed to matter, but they did.

A stupid story my mother told, the things she said about me but not about Jena—that wasn't supposed to matter, either.

Does it matter?

Am I the girl with nine lives?

I try to hold my breath, because it can't be true. But there's only one way to know for sure if Mom was right about me.

The lump in my throat rises and threatens to consume me. Moisture seeps into my ankles, melted snow on my socks.

I follow my feet behind the house, to the icy square lake that also functions as a pool. Peeling off my wet socks but keeping on my jeans, I pull back the pool cover and stick my toes in the water. It feels like a million little bites, a thousand bitter stabs, freezing, burning, scalding, cold.

Am I the girl with nine lives?

I lower myself into the water. All of me. And sink into it, gritting my teeth as I push myself underwater. Then I stay, fighting the urge to come up for air. Waiting, waiting, is this going to work, when will they find me, my brain is cold, I'm so sleepy, I can't think. I've been under here too long.

I am the girl with nine lives. Or six, because of the car accident. Because of the chest infection. Because of this.

The floor of this pool would have pulled Jena to the bottom, sucking all the air from her lungs. She would have drowned.

I have to be the girl with nine lives, because I *did* just drown, and now, I'm back.

six
six

8

What the hell did you think you were doing?" my mother fumes as she stands behind me on her bed. A million blankets are bundled around me, and she's towel-drying my hair. I feel like a wet dog and suddenly I get this urge to shake, shake, shake all the water off me. But I am too tired.

She's been yelling at me for quite some time now. Yelling and sniffing, switching between Parenting Technique One: I'm all ears and just tell me how you *feel*, and Parenting Technique Two: You're damn lucky I don't believe in corporal punishment.

After finding and pulling me out of the pool, Dad has wisely made himself scarce. He's been "checking on Jena" for the past half hour.

"Well?" Mom keeps saying, and waiting for me to talk. I still feel cold. It's a chill that eats away at the inside of me so the blankets don't matter. I've been shivering for nearly an hour now. I am so tired.

"How am I supposed to help you if you won't talk to me?" Mom asks.

She doesn't remember what she's said all these years, that her words stayed with me when they weren't supposed to.

I am the girl with nine lives.

"I'm sorry," I finally say.

She stops drying my hair and gets me another blanket and socks for my feet.

"You can sleep in here tonight," she says. It's not an option. My behavior has demoted me to sleeping in my parents' bedroom. I want to argue or run to my own room while her back is turned. I'll draw skulls and crossbones on the door so she knows she can't enter. But I don't feel like me. So I lie down and fall asleep.

I still feel cold. I feel even more tired.

I think I'm morphing into Jena.

Jena is awake and her fever is gone and she's keeping down food.

Sometime in between me drowning and waking up this morning, Jena started to feel better.

I know she is still sick. Sunken brown rings swallow up her eyes, her skin is cool and yellow, and her hair is patchy on the left side. But I drowned, and today, she's better. Maybe, just maybe, like the cats Uncle Stephan talked about, if I lose enough lives, one of them will float back down to her. Maybe one of them will make her well.

I can't stop fidgeting and my heart thunders around in my chest, but I try to look calm.

We spend our Sunday curled up on opposite ends of a sofa that is much too big for her alone and much too small for the both of us, watching television. Jena and I are covered in the same number of blankets.

Almost all the ones on top of me, which Mom dug out from the back of the linen closet, belonged to my grandmother, and soon, everywhere smells like her.

"I'm getting a refill. Anyone want more hot chocolate?" Dad asks.

I hold up my mug for him.

Only the three of us are home today, since Mom is off posing as an evangelical Christian somewhere. She was hesitant to leave, but Dad insisted that he had everything under control. I guess his show of heroism—namely, pulling me out of the pool—convinced her enough that she actually agreed. And true to his word, my father hasn't let me and my sister out of his sight all morning. He keeps squeezing my shoulder, and sometimes he stares at me like he wants to say something. Like he's trying to figure me out.

I rest my head against the back of the sofa and glance at the clock. Two more hours till I can take another Advil. It just figures that I die and wake up with the world's worst hangover.

"Pass me the remote," Jena says. I crawl out from the layers of cloth and reach for the remote.

Without a word (e.g., *thanks*), she takes it from me and starts flicking. Not many people are Team Dani today.

Dad's done such a good job watching us so far that we haven't had a chance to switch to a decent channel, and the situation's a bit desperate since we've been watching the Cartoon Network all day. Apparently he still thinks that's our favorite.

"Okay, here you go." He returns with two steaming cups of hot chocolate and places one on the table in front of me. Then he sits back and rips open a bag of pistachio nuts. "Sure you don't want anything, Jena?"

"No, thanks."

"Hey, who changed it to the Game Show Network?"

Jena doesn't answer him, and neither do I.

A few minutes later, the phone rings and Dad goes to pick it up. It's Mom.

"Of course they are." Pause. "No, everything is fine. It's just . . . you know how they are when they're sick."

"It's true," Jena says. "You're always pissed off when you're hungover."

I turn to face her, keeping an even expression. "How many times do I have to say it? I just needed some fresh air. I was taking a walk outside and—"

"You wanted to feel the water," she cuts in. "And once you had the pool cover off, you leaned over too far and fell in." Her voice is acerbic, knowing. "Now tell me, would this have anything to do with the fact that you were beyond wasted?"

"I don't know what you're talking about." I'm not paying

much attention to our conversation; I'm thinking about cats and drowning and the fact that she doesn't have a fever today. I wonder how long it will last. How many good days am I worth?

She harrumphs. "I smelled you, idiot. Great idea capitalizing on the whole I-just-leaned-over-to-check-on-the-propellers shit from *Titanic*, though. Too bad it was as stupid an excuse then as it is now."

Dad is coming back in, and I say much too loudly, "Jenavieve, please don't swear. Mom's off appealing for a pity vote from God, remember?"

She glares at me. Dad resumes his seat and looks between the two of us, feigning exasperation. "What's wrong now?"

"You wouldn't understand," I answer tiredly.

"Aw, come on," Dad pushes. "Try me." Neither of us answers. We zone out and continue to watch *The Weakest Link*. Jena has always loved game shows. That's one thing that hasn't changed.

Dad says it's because of her competitive spirit, the one she inherited from him. But while she watches with unmerited interest, he falls asleep with his mouth open about halfway through our second episode. It might be because he was up too late or too early last night or this morning. Personally, I think it means Jena better look into finding her birth parents.

On Monday morning, debate ensues as to whether or not I should go to school, but we are all too tired to fight. I want to go. Being buried under shovelfuls of cotton and yarn, with the smell of my parents and grandmother hovering over me constantly, is not my idea of fun.

My father apparently feels better if he drops me at my bus stop, which is less than a block away from our house, on his way to work. During the wait for the bus, I stuff my hands in the pockets of my jeans and think.

Three lives down, six to go.

The bus turns up eventually and I climb on, locate my usual spot at the back, and lean into the cool glass of the window.

Once we get to school, I climb off the bus and head right to math class.

Is it just me, or is everything painfully repetitive?

"Jack, how sweet of you to save me a seat." I slide into the empty chair beside him and beam over at him. Seeing him here, clutching the corners of his textbook like a life raft and trying to ignore me, feels infinitely more normal than running into him at that party on Saturday. But that could well be due to the conspicuously absent jaundiced glow of the kitchen.

Lauren leans over and announces, "I've never been more happy to see a person in my life. I was sure you were dead."

"Me too, Lauren," I say. "Me too." She assumes I am joking and laughs.

Mr. Halbrook taps a couple of times on the whiteboard, the universal signal that he actually has something to teach today. And he's serious.

As it turns out, we're getting a project and we're to work in pairs.

"It's about math," he says, striding across the room with his arms tucked into each other behind his back. I'm impressed already. "There is history to everything. Even to your beloved Internet and text messages."

If people are meant to stop texting, a handful miss this vital piece of information. If we are supposed to laugh, we also miss that memo.

Halbrook continues, "Most people fail to realize that math, yes, mathematics, has a history. And your assignment, if you choose to accept it . . ."

"Oh God," Lauren whispers to me. She's frantically scribbling in her notebook and I presume her panic has less to do with the fact that we have a nut for a teacher—okay, not a nut; he just really badly wants to be in the Oval Office, apparently—and more to do with the fact that she missed the last word in his speech.

". . . is to create a chronology of mathematics."

There are plenty of sighs now, some murmurs, complaints. Halbrook dedicates the rest of the period to doing damage control and, at the very end, makes sure everyone has a partner.

Lauren pairs off with Rachel Talbot, this girl who was expelled from her old school for protesting staff use of student microwaves. I think they'll work well together.

"So, how about it, pardner?" I say, addressing Jack.

"Uh, actually," he stutters. "Toby probably wants to work together."

I glance over my shoulder. "Looks like Toby already has a

partner. That cheating piece of scum," I add with a wink. Jack doesn't appear to share my enthusiasm.

Mr. Halbrook's gray-speckled eyebrows dart up a bit when I inform him that Jack and I will be working together. Maybe it's because I refer to us as "a couple." Either way, he sends Jack a sympathetic glance.

As we're packing up at the end of the period, Jack suddenly turns to me and says, "You have to pull your weight."

"Of course." I smile.

He hesitates, like he can't decide whether now is the time for an I'm-going-to-an-Ivy-League-school-and-grades-may-not-be-important-to-you-but...speech. Evidently he decides against it, because soon just his back is in the doorway, kids from next period are starting to file in, and there's a chance I've been standing here for too long.

9

"Guess what? You'll never guess!"

"What, Mom?" She nearly knocks me over when I walk through the front door after school. My heart jumps out of its cage to see what the fuss is about. Damn thing. Always so hopeful, but my voice hides it well. I'm trying to see behind Mom to find Jena. To see if she's still better, if that's what Mom is so excited about.

"You got a callback for the commercial! They left a message this morning while Jena and I were at her appointment and they said they really liked what you did. They like *you*."

My heart goes sulking back into its little compartment, and tucks itself somewhere far away where it can crystallize and become a fossil.

"Mom!" I shriek. "That's great!"

"I know." She pulls me against herself and then tears me away to cup my face in her hands. "You see? I told you it would finally happen for you."

How do I tell her that a Whitaden commercial does not a

Happen make? I mean, it's better than school plays, but it's nothing to write home about. My mother thrives on excitement, though, and, given that the pool incident ruined her weekend, I figure I can allow her this.

"This is so exciting," I gush as we enter the living room. I see Jena sitting at the dining room table with a plate of something tofu-related and a glass of cranberry juice in front of her. She manages to look both miserable on account of herself and skeptical on account of me and my enthusiasm.

She's wearing an old violet beanie, her favorite one, and an oversized blue hoodie. From what I can tell, she's had a decent day.

I turn back to Mom. "So what else did they say?"

"Well, the callback is this Saturday. They'll let us know about the actual filming depending on how callbacks go. Jena, you've barely touched your food!"

I'm glad that the attention is momentarily off me as my sister tries to convince Mom that *yes, she's fine* and *no, she doesn't feel sick* and *she just doesn't feel like eating*. I will her to say it feistily, like she means it.

But the sound of a fork unhappily scraping a plate reminds me that the Jena I know is too sleepy to come out and someone, something, has taken her place, pretending to be my sister and not doing a very convincing job. Why do we let her get away with it?

At dinner, when Dad gets home, we talk a lot about the commercial. It's only the three of us because Jena's taking a nap, but Mom's excitement is enough to fill a fourth place just for tonight.

Dad beams and tries not to say straight out that he had a role in this success. Mom talks about other "opportunities for us" that she's come across lately.

"I've just been so scatterbrained that I haven't made any phone calls or set up anything yet."

"Honey, I can call if you want."

She considers this for a second. "No, it's probably better if I call. Besides, with you filling in as Danielle's manager, this is the least I can do to feel like I'm even part of her budding career," Mom jokes. Except it's not totally a joke. She wishes she was doing auditions, not radiation.

"Please," Dad answers modestly. "All I did was take her to one audition . . . although I did feel confident that she had it in the bag. Didn't I tell you?"

My mother used to be in musicals before she met my father. All sorts of theater productions and acting gigs—one of which, apparently, led to her becoming bosom buddies with Brody Richardson. After busting her knee during a matinee of *My Fair Lady*, she had to take a final bow of sorts. At the time, of course, it was only supposed to be temporary. She wasn't supposed to fall in love with a big-hearted dork from New Jersey (my dad) and get knocked up—with twins.

So you could say her heart never really left the stage. And that's where I come in.

Some people say I seem like a natural actress, but that could easily be that thing that happens when you've been told you're one thing your entire life so you become it. Or maybe I am.

All I know is that, through no fault of my own, my mother and I have always been eerily similar—the acting, the near-deaths—while she and Jena were pretty much opposites.

10

The history of math. That's such a broad topic," Jack says. Halbrook has relocated math class to the library on Tuesday so we can start working on our assignments.

From his seat beside me, Jack stares at me, an unreadable expression on his face. I pull out the end of the yellow pencil from between my upper and lower molars. "Sorry. Was this yours?"

He doesn't take the pencil I'm holding out, and I eventually place it on the desk, where it leaves a print of saliva and Danielle germs.

"I don't even know where to start," Jack says, and I'm a little surprised to note that his voice is slightly deeper than I'd thought. "It's so ambiguous."

I nod thoughtfully, opening up my notebook. "Well, I worried that you'd overthink this assignment—no offense. So I took matters into my own hands." I pull out a pile of printed papers.

Jack lifts the first sheet and stares at it for a long time.

"I Googled 'math.'" I beam at him. "I think we're set."

He lowers the piece of paper. "I'm not sure this is what he was asking for. Besides, isn't this Infopedia site supposed to be unreliable? Anybody can put in information."

"And that makes it unreliable? That's prejudice."

Jack flips through the rest of the papers. Finally he says, "Well, it still doesn't really answer Mr. Halbrook's questions."

"God."

"What?"

"God," I repeat. "That's his answer."

Jack stares at me. "I don't understand."

"Where did math start?" I lean back till the front two legs of my chair rise up and the weight of the chair and me depend entirely on the wooden bookcase behind us. This isn't technically allowed in the school library, but Mrs. Uri, our librarian, has her back to us. The only other class in here apart from our math class is the senior gym class, meaning a) resident hot P.E. teacher, Mr. Thomas, is here too, and b) Mrs. Uri will be directing all that austere energy toward protecting the paperbacks from sweat and athlete's foot.

"Everything supposedly starts with God, correct? So did math."

"Do you want me to write that down?" I ask when Jack makes no move to do so himself. "To be honest," I lean in toward him and whisper conspiratorially, "I'm fairly certain that *that's* the answer to all of Halbrook's problems. Religion. It

~ 60

will help him find himself, make peace with the past and let go of his failed dreams and all that . . . It helped my mom."

Skipping breakfast once again has caught up with me, and my stomach growls its disapproval. I rummage through my backpack and pull out a half-empty bag of Doritos. They've been under my books since yesterday, so the chips are more like chiplets. "Want some?" Moist, sticky, tiny, delicious chiplets.

Jack's eyes scan the library nervously. "No, thanks." I wonder if it's getting caught with the chips he's anxious about, or the fact that he has me for a partner.

"Um, thanks for going to the trouble of printing this—"

"No trouble," I shrug.

"—but we don't actually . . . I think we'll probably have to go more in-depth with this. Maybe we could even go to the public library and do some research."

Mrs. Uri's head suddenly snaps in our direction. Perhaps I've been too loud with the chips.

Her eyes lock on mine, willing me into a puddle of molten teenager. I don't look away. A second later, she's leaving her desk and heading across the room toward me, toward us.

"Sure you don't want any?" I slide the crumpled packet toward Jack. He doesn't have time to protest.

Mrs. Uri stops in front of us. She opens her mouth to speak, to yell and foam and teacher-curse the day I was born. Then, her face softens and the side of her mouth crumples. "Hi, Danielle."

"Hi?"

She is still smiling, but her eyes travel to the table and the offending bag o' chips. "You and Jenavieve—"

"Jena."

"—Jenny—"

"*Jena.*"

"—look so much alike. I mean, for nonidentical—"

"Fraternal," says Jack.

"—twins," finishes Mrs. Uri. She keeps smiling at me, waiting: won't I thank her? Being told you look like someone else is supposed to be the ultimate compliment, and yet it never really feels like it. Especially when it isn't true. It's just that seeing me reminds her of Jena.

She can't ignore the shiny chip bag anymore, and without looking at it, as if swiping a fly in her periphery or overcome by a tick, she slams her hand down on the table and wraps it in her palm. "You can't eat in here, Danielle. Please don't make me tell you again."

Still smiling, she turns, going back to her task of paperback sweat prevention.

"I'm leaving," I announce as soon as she's gone.

Jack holds out a single finger at me. "You were going to pretend it was mine."

"So if you don't like my information, feel free to find your own. From, like, *reliable sources.*" I stuff my mostly empty notebook into my backpack and hesitate. Who gets custody of the chewed-on, salivary yellow pencil?

"I can't believe you'd do that."

Withholding a groan, I throw the pencil into my backpack. Hurt is so not sexy on a nerd.

"Sweetie," I coo, "relax, she didn't say anything about expelling either one of us."

Jack stands with me now and, leaving his stuff on the table, follows me out of the library. Mr. Halbrook is talking to Mrs. Uri. With her luck, he's the one hitting on her—not resident hot P.E. teacher, Mr. Thomas. I bet she's playing the "I'm married" card. Either way, Jack and I get out unnoticed.

"But you tried to make it look like I was the one eating them."

I wait till we're safely through the library doors before I tiredly face Jack. "A bag of chips? Really? Of all the things to come between us."

Jack starts to say something else, but I cut him off. "Look, she *saw* me inhaling the pack beforehand. She *saw* me slide it over to you. She *knew* it was me."

"Then why did you do it?"

Feeling frustrated at Jack's complete fixation and psychological inertia, I turn and walk down the length of the hall. It's barely the start of the day, but the thought of another two periods of pointless conversations before lunch, not to mention my chemistry teacher lecturing in monotone, seems unbearable. I figure a little break won't hurt.

Backpack in hand, I slip out the heavy iron doors leading to the front of the school. If we were some New York City school, we might have security guards traipsing the halls or

X-ray machines that beep when we have something forbidden. Or swipe cards that ensure that we are doing what we should be doing when we should be doing it. But we are not some New York City school, and if we skip out during school hours, we will only have Our Consciences to answer to and Our Parents' Voicemails to delete and Our Bad Grades to be ashamed of. I'm surprised I don't run into the entire student body outside the school doors.

Well, let them sit inside in the warmth with their flattened Dorito chip bags hidden between their textbooks, and their bags of candy in opened backpacks where they can slip their fingers in and get their sugar fix. Me? I prefer the cold.

I head to the football field behind the school building. In the distance, a group of freshmen (led by the *other* P.E. teacher and non-hottie, Mr. Kelton) alternate between jogging half-heartedly around the field, navigating clumped pockets of un-melted snow, and making out with asthma puffers. Today is warmer than it's been in weeks, but it's still early February. I'm pretty sure forcing kids to run laps qualifies as cruel and un-usual punishment. I find a nook of the building where I can watch them, but they can't see me. Then I drop my backpack on the ground and sit on top of it.

Mr. Kelton blows a shrill whistle and the class assembles in the middle of the field. My eyes skim over them, to the soc-cer goalpost way over at the end of the field.

It's been forever since I watched a soccer game.

I hate soccer. The fact that it's outdoors. The excessive

celebration after a goal. The head-butting. The fact that an en-tire near-two-hours of match time can go by without a single goal.

I don't miss it.

But it reminds me of hearing about which boy came to watch which game they were playing. Of Jena's obnoxious cleat stomp-dance, of tripping over gym bags and balls in our hallway at home. Of a time when I was allowed to openly hate soccer, because you can hate things you're sure of, things that aren't going away.

A scrawny freshman is doubled over, red-faced and clutch-ing his side, but a tuft of vapor drifts out of his mouth, assuring me that he is alive. His friend stops jogging to walk alongside him, and little clouds sail out of his mouth too as he speaks. The whole freshman class is breathing, all of them releasing malformed air letters to rub it in that they are alive.

I am, too. I breathe through my mouth. Staring over at the deserted soccer post, treacherously declaring that I am alive. I clamp my mouth shut and my throat constricts.

I want to evaporate.

If Jena and I were just sisters, not twins, it wouldn't matter that I couldn't donate blood or stem cells or bone marrow to her. But I am her twin and I still can't.

I pull my knees up, rest my head on them, and shut my eyes. I'm trying to empty my mind, trying to lull myself to sleep. It feels like it's working for the first thirty seconds, until I hear some shuffling and snow crunching around me. Without lifting my head, I see a pair of ratty white sneakers, with a grass stain on the left one. Above them are a pair of skinny-boy legs hidden beneath skinny-boy black pants, which are a little short for my taste.

"Are you okay?" Jack asks. Since I last saw him, he's put on a dark green coat. He's staring down at me, looking uncomfortable. "After our . . . dispute, I saw you come outside. So as soon as math ended, I wanted to come and find you."

He exhales and I'm mesmerized by his smoky breath.

"Oh."

"I wanted to apologize," Jack continues. "For before, I mean. I realize I overreacted."

"I'd forgotten all about it," I say, pulling myself up and wiping my palms on the back of my jeans.

"As long as you don't hate me," Jack says.

"I could never." I poke my elbow into his side. For once I don't have the energy to tease him, to be the Dani he knows. I heave my backpack onto my shoulder. "We better get back inside."

The last person I expect to see when I come out of the school building at the end of the day is my father. He's parked by the curb, behind a snail trail of school buses. Dad waves manically, while I try to think of some way I can get away with pretending not to know him. Amnesia, maybe?

"Dani!"

I take my time walking toward the car.

"I knocked off a few hours early, so I thought I'd spare you the bus ride."

"Thanks, Dad," I say, climbing into the passenger seat.

My heart sinks when he doesn't immediately start the car.

"I've been thinking," he begins, his hand placed on the steering wheel, TV-dad style, "you just . . . you haven't seemed like yourself lately—which is understandable. I mean, we all feel *different*. But I know you've been taking all this pretty hard and I . . . what I mean is . . . Do you think you're . . . Are you worried about getting . . . cancer?"

Even now, it's still hard for him to say it. I don't blame him. It's an icky word. Why couldn't whoever was in charge of naming things call cancer "sugar" and sugar "cancer"? People might not eat so much of the stuff then. And it's so much more pleasant to die of sugar.

Before I can speak, he rushes on. "Because it makes sense why you might think that, with you and Jena being twins. But as Dr. Thames explained back in July, the likelihood of your getting sick is pretty low. You don't need to worry about that."

He pauses now, waiting for me to confirm that this is, in fact, what is wrong.

"I get it," I say. "Whatever I die from probably won't be cancer. Maybe I'll get hit by a UFO. Ooh, or one of those freak rollercoaster-ride-gone-wrong deals."

"Dani—"

"Dad, it's freezing in here. Do you want me to die of frostbite?"

"No," he says, "I don't want you to die of anything." I stare straight ahead, my throat lumpy, as I begin to think he really is just going to make us sit here and "talk." But he starts the car and pulls out onto the road. "So, your mom and I were looking at some RVs in the paper the other day. To rent for August."

I relax and melt into my seat. "Yeah?"

"Yeah." He launches into the story, lamenting prices and filling every seat in the car, except mine, with excitement over the trip he and Mom had been planning for last August. When it didn't happen, my parents acted like it had nothing to do with Jena's diagnosis, like the plans just fell through, but we all know the truth. "So that's the one we're leaning toward right now. It would have to be in the summer, of course."

The rest of the way home, we talk about school and Dad's work and our elusive trip and that callback of mine.

When he found me in the pool the other night, Dad scolded me for not being careful and asked if I'd had anything to drink, even though he had to have smelled it on me.

He thinks I'm acting out because I'm scared of getting sick.

What would he think if he knew that Mom was right about my lives, if he knew that I *could* help Jena after all?

I know having nine lives (or six) falls under the category of Impossible Things, things that you are committed to scary institutions for believing.

But she only needs one, and six lives are too many for any one person.

11

I've had an epiphany." Lauren flops down next to me on a bench in the cafeteria. I've decided to take the day off from sitting with Spencer and Candy.

"An epiphany," I repeat slowly, twirling a piece of lettuce around my fork and willing myself to eat it. Mom was preoccupied this morning, so I threw together the only non-tofu meal I could think of—a salad. Jena's done with radiation for the foreseeable future, but they have a meeting with her oncologist this afternoon, an "update," which is almost worse. Even Jena was nervous this morning.

I've been sitting here for the past five minutes, trying to figure out whether salads are always this brown, or if it's just me.

"It's, like, a revelation. A sudden realization. When something you haven't—"

"I know what an epiphany is," I tell Lauren.

"Oh. Well, yesterday," she continues, "it hit me that I've been living in total complacency. I've allowed myself to become yet another self-absorbed, shallow adolescent. It's sickening."

No, the fact that my lunch looks like it might be alive is.

I glance at the huge wall clock across the cafeteria. *12:10.*

"I mean, so many people all around the world are voiceless. Unable to express their opinions and be heard, and yet *we* all sit here silent and immobile. Sickening," she says again, with a shake of her head. Her sandwich is wrapped in blue, grease-resistant paper, and the smell of Marmite assaults my senses as soon as she opens it up. Her sister, Nicole, introduced her to Marmite after she got back from doing fieldwork in New Zealand, and Lauren has been obsessed ever since.

For the next ten minutes, Lauren rambles on about her epiphany and how, from here on out, she refuses to stay silent. I stare at her sandwich as she speaks. Somehow it manages to look way more appetizing than my salad, even though I think Marmite tastes like earwax.

"Did you know that when she was nine, Rachel Talbot staged a protest by sitting in this ancient tree at her elementary school when they tried to cut it down? Stuff like that just makes me feel so inspired."

"So she's a tree hugger?" I ask, finally giving up and pushing away my salad. *12:21.*

Lauren frowns. "I've always found that term derogatory. She's a passionate campaigner concerned with environmental causes."

Lauren keeps talking, hardly stopping for a breath. Most people don't have all that much to say to me. The brave ones risk a "how are you," but it's not long before even they realize that there's a long list of words they can't mention in front of me: sister, sick, time, hair, hospital, eyebrows . . . After a while, no matter how brave you are, you realize it's just easier not to talk.

But Lauren's in a world of her own. That first week after we found out about Jena, the phone rang incessantly—people we barely knew spewing *words of encouragement* and well wishes and ifthere'sanythingwecandos, until someone took the phone off the hook. Before that, though, Lauren called. It was uncharacteristic—she hardly ever calls me—and I braced myself for whatever profound but useless thing she was going to add to the many we'd heard. But she didn't say anything. Not one word. We sat there in silence for five minutes, and then I said I had to go, and that was it. Those five minutes were all we've ever said about Jena.

These days, since I have less to say—and because she *can*—she greedily swallows all the empty silences, the commas, the periods, and the question marks. I guess she just has a lot to say. Or maybe she does it because she doesn't like the way air swishes around in your eardrums when nobody says anything, and so she fills the silence with too many words.

"I just feel like I'm ready to make a big difference, you know?"

I nod. *12:30.* Half an hour before Jena's appointment.

"By the way, have you ever noticed that classrooms are practically a dictatorship? I hadn't either, until I started talking to Rachel. I mean, I was skeptical at first, but think about it—we start class when the teacher gets there, we stop when he's ready to stop, assessments are totally up to the teacher. They say we have a test on Monday, and we have to take a test on Monday. I say, Enough is enough."

Before, when Lauren used to get all passionate like this, I would try to avoid her. There's just something about her franticness that stresses people out. But now, her speech is calming. It plays like background music to my thoughts, something normal and familiar. My eyes float across the room to the table closest to the cafeteria line.

Ben Hershey, Khy, and Erin are sitting together again, and this time Ben has on his basketball uniform. I barely used to notice them last year, but now I'm constantly looking over, waiting for them to miss her.

Lauren doesn't speak for a second, and when I look back at her, she's staring at me, one eyebrow raised.

"What's wrong?" she asks.

"Nothing."

"You should really consider what I'm saying," Lauren says. "You're complacent, too. I mean, what do you care about?"

"I don't know," I tell her, and swallow to make my throat less tight.

"Exactly. You should really figure it out, Dani. Or you'll become just like everybody else."

Right then, Erin turns and looks over her shoulder. For a split second, she looks annoyed, since I'm not trying to hide the fact that I'm staring. But then she turns back around and keeps on eating her lunch.

Lauren is still talking, because she gets to worry about that: being *unique*, making a difference, and the politically correct term for hugging trees.

We're so different, I don't even know why we're friends.

"Where have you been?" Mom corners me as soon as I step into the house. "It's six-thirty."

"I was at the public library," I say, and it should be a lie, but it's not. I took the bus there after school, found a quiet corner, and fell asleep reading a book ingeniously titled *Felines, Our Friends*. I didn't want to be home alone if I got here before they did, and then I didn't want to know if there was bad news. "I have this big math assignment."

"That is unacceptable, Dani. Is it too much to ask that you tell people where you're going?" Mom rants.

"Sorry." Avoiding her eye, I ask, "How did the meeting go?"

Mom sighs, and I can hear the tiredness in her voice. "Well. Her blood work could have been better. He wasn't thrilled with her white blood cell count." She starts spewing numbers, and I wonder if now is a good time to tell her I'm this close to failing math. The bottom line is that we're still waiting on a marrow match.

I leave Mom calling Dad to inform him that I've been found.

Jena's not on the couch, not in the kitchen, not at the dining room table. I go upstairs to look for her, just to double-check that she still exists. I wait outside her room, my ear pressed against her door. If it's something I don't want to see, then I won't go in. If it's completely silent, then I haven't decided what I'll do yet.

I'm not sure what it is exactly, but I hear *something*, so I turn the handle and start to go in. I have to push the door open all the way before I see her, crouched down, on her knees in front of her closet.

"Are you praying?" I don't mean to sound so incredulous; it's just . . .

I take a couple steps forward. No, she's not praying. There's music playing in the background, something metallic and fraught with swear words, except it's on so low, it might as well not be.

"What are you doing?"

"Turn it off," Jena commands.

I don't pretend not to know what she's talking about. Instead, I cross the room, head toward the stereo, and press the "off" button. This is just like old times, her bossing me around and me doing it.

Loud, thick, and anxious breathing fills the room in place of the music, and I'm about to yell for whoever it is to stop, when I realize it's me.

"My closet's a mess," Jena says after a second, holding up a pair of sweatpants. She sounds normal, and it's true. Her closet is a mess. There are piles of clothes on the floor. Except the hangers are down with them, like someone pulled them down.

Angry music. A demolished closet.

Angry music, but soft. A demolished closet, but she's cleaning it. Her movements are slow and floppy, and I can tell she's exhausted.

"I'll give you fifty bucks if you help me."

"You don't have fifty bucks."

"I have twenty," she says. "Dad gave it to me."

"What for?" I ask. Because here I was under the impression that I was Dad's new favorite, since Jena is Mom's.

"I don't know. It's not like I don't still spend money."

She's holding up a T-shirt that is too big for her. It always was, but it must have enlarged and stretched in the wash. Why else would it look so huge against her body?

Then she takes it and tucks the sleeves in, folds it down the middle and in half, the way Mom does.

"Why don't you just leave it till later, if you're tired? Or Mom could do it for you." Really, I mean: if you went to all the trouble of pulling down all the hangers in your closet and kicking around your shoes and slamming your hand in the wall—I can't find the dent, but I know it's here somewhere—and playing your pretentious and angry underground-band music, why didn't you do it properly? Why didn't you leave it? Why are you Jena-halfway some of the time, and not my sister Jena all of the time?

"The mess was driving me insane."

Liar, I don't say.

"So will you help me?" Jena asks.

I pick up a pair of shorts and start folding. *Of course I will help you. I will help you back down and cower and hide the fact that you're secretly pissed about this whole being-sick thing, but not really sure how to show it. I will help you pack up the mess you made for what we both know is a false sense of accomplishment. That sense of "God, Jena, but you are such a badass. You made a little mess in the back of your closet where no one can see it? Bad. Ass."*

She's wearing a multicolored beanie, the edges pulled down tight over her ears, because her ears are always cold, even inside.

I get on my knees and start folding. Beside me, Jena keeps moving slowly, breathing loud.

"I want that twenty," I tell her as I stuff a folded shirt into the back of her closet.

While we're cleaning up, one thought runs through my mind, makes me feel better. I can help her.

I'm still on number six.

12

Dad drops me off at school early on Thursday morning and, I have to admit, words cannot describe the satisfaction that arises from being the first person there. There's something invigorating about being first at anything, especially if you take full advantage of it and sit at the entrance, staring down people like they're late as they come inside.

There's also the fact that I beat Lauren to math class, which is basically unheard of. Her lateness, however, gives me a chance to sit back, fold my arms across my chest, and admire the hotness that is Jack Penner. When he glances at me uncomfortably from the corner of his eyes, I even tell him so.

"Sorry," I say, leaning forward in my chair. "I just forget everything when I look at you."

He's gotten pretty good at pretending not to have heard me, but the way his cheeks redden like overripe tomatoes always gives him away.

"I think we should meet at the library to work on our

assignment next week," Jack says, refusing to meet my eye. "We didn't get very much done last time."

"I know, it was really unfortunate," I agree, even though I'm still harboring a lot of hurt over the fact that he rejected the ideas I presented. And almost let a bag of chips ruin what we have.

Halbrook announces that we're watching a movie he hopes will inspire us for our assignments. And for a second, we are hopeful. Today's class might not be a total bust.

Then, he brings out an ancient-looking video and VCR.

Many heads hit desks, and palms embrace cell phones.

I'm more open-minded, so I'm willing to give it a chance—that is, until black-and-white figures begin to scurry across the screen, robotic and scratchy-voiced. Then I'm done.

I notice that Rachel Talbot is sitting by herself in the row beside ours, unwrapping a Fruit Roll-Up beneath her desk, and I wonder aloud if Lauren is sick.

"Didn't you get the e-mail?" Jack whispers back.

"E-mail?" I forgot I had that.

He nods. "About the walkout. Lauren's staging a walkout for eight-forty."

I glance at the clock. It's eight thirty-five. "Why is everybody still here, then?"

Jack shrugs. "I guess they're not going. It wasn't really clear what exactly we were supposed to be protesting. Plus, it sounds like trouble."

I think back to the conversation Lauren and I had yesterday.

About her wanting to *speak out* and *be heard*. It really looks like she's going to be the only one at her own walkout, and I can't help but feel a little bad for her.

Just seeing an e-mail with sender "Lauren Friedman" would probably be enough to get half the student body to delete it. The other half might or might not read it, and those who do are hardly going to stick out their necks to support her political agenda. What I don't understand, though, is why she's not here, but Rachel Talbot is. I mean, isn't Rachel supposed to be her mentor or something? Her new political adviser? The girl that is a cause before a person?

But here she sits, slumped in her chair, watching the grainy black-and-white video. She's on to her second Fruit Roll-Up.

There's something wrong with this picture.

"Are we supposed to be taking notes?" Lance Hutchinson, the only other kid watching apart from Rachel—even Jack is reading a book—asks, raising his head.

Of course Halbrook says, "Yes. All material presented in class is testable."

And I want to pummel Lance because a) I've always had unhealthy aggression issues, and b) you should never give teachers the chance to say, "I told you it was testable."

It doesn't matter, though, because nobody moves to pull their notebooks out, and Halbrook himself is reading *Time* magazine behind his desk.

I rest my head on my desk and determine that if I wasn't

so lazy, I'd probably join Lauren. The "academic discipline" our student handbook refers to has to beat watching this video.

Lauren is back by lunch, her lips forming one thin, angry line. She flops down across from me at a table in the cafeteria.

"I hate this school," she announces.

"I know," I say, determined to be understanding and supportive of her failed mission. "You were right. We're all very complacent."

"What?" she says, opening a container of blueberry yogurt. "Well, yes, you are. But what I mean is I hate this *school*. They are running a complete autocracy." She dips her spoon into the yogurt and shakes her head. "Do you know that they tried to sabotage the walkout? I don't know how they found out about it. Rachel thinks they probably hack into our e-mail."

"Why was Rachel in class, by the way?" I ask. "During the walkout?"

"She couldn't do it because she's already on a tight rope. If she gets kicked out of Quentin, she'll have to be homeschooled. And her parents are apparently really psycho and think the world is flat."

It's not? "Well, that sucks."

Lauren nods. "Anyway, I have detention for skipping class. *Detention*." Something about her voice suggests she cares more than she's letting on. Lauren Friedman doesn't get detention. Ever. And although she's trying to act like she's forgotten who she is, she still remembers.

"I'm going to get my parents to call Principal Motley."

Forgetting yourself is probably the hardest part of changing who you are. But if that's true, then there's something wrong with me. I remember specific things—what I wore when I auditioned for *Oklahoma!* two years ago; that I placed third in Quentin's spelling bee in sixth grade—but I barely remember who I *was*, if I even existed, before.

13

On Saturday, the morning of my callback, I wake up early to the smell of vomit and bleach. From my position in bed, I hear the sound of footsteps, desperate and heavy on the other side of the door.

Next comes a loud silence in which I try to breathe quietly. All I hear is the sound of the tiny white fan in Mom and Dad's room, the one reserved for sticky summers and heat waves, beating and swiping angrily at the air.

Are we all holding our breaths?

Then the sound of her retching. A violent, gurgling noise that seems to come from someplace deeper, more hollow than her stomach. I close my eyes so I don't have to imagine it.

Make it stop. I wish someone would make her stop.

She keeps doing it, and our house shakes with the loudness. My father charges up and down the stairs, delivering my mother's orders of *a glass of cold water, Eric* and *her tablets, Eric! You know the ones, the ones she takes. The ones she always takes.* I imagine his knees kicking up close to his jaw from the effort when he runs. Maybe he's dressed in green and gold jogging gear, with a matching headband. Maybe he trips over his own feet on his way down the stairs.

It's quiet for a few minutes, and then Jena is back at it.

"Again?" My mother's voice breaks and falls apart on itself. "On *what*, Eric? She hasn't eaten anything."

Dad mutters something soothing and comforting, and I wonder if it's actually helping or just freaking Mom out.

A couple of minutes later, the door of my room opens, a trail of blue light from the hallway traveling in. I freeze, my eyes shut. I don't want them to know I'm awake.

"Dani?" Dad brushes a strand of hair from my face and nudges me gently. "Dani, your mother and I are taking Jena to the hospital."

I know I can't keep pretending now. I have to say something. Maybe to Jena. At the very least to Dad.

Is she going to be okay?

Should I come?

"What about my callback?" That's what I say.

Dad swears softly. "I'd forgotten about that. I don't think we'll make it. I'll call you from the hospital and let you know what the plan is, okay?"

"Yeah." Other words rise and fall between us. They scurry into the darkness, the farthest corners of my room. I can't make my lips move.

"SHIT!" More retching. My mother's feet urgently moving across the carpet downstairs. "Eric?"

He places a kiss on my forehead. "Try to get some sleep, okay?"

I don't answer and then he's gone and I'm left in the darkness with the words I can't make myself say.

My mind won't let me sleep so I lie there, breathing in the vomit-tainted air, the smell of too much bleach, the odor of dying sisters. And I'm still on number six.

I pull the covers over my head to make it stop.

They've been gone a couple of hours when I leave.

The ride downtown takes just over half an hour and then I'm stepping off the bus and walking toward Heaven's Cycle. The store is located in the most deserted part of downtown, the place where all the crimes and muggings take place. It also happens to be where Spencer works.

"Hey!" He is surprised but pleased to see me. He comes around from behind the counter to meet me. "What are you doing here?"

"I was just in the neighborhood."

An eyebrow goes up as an unbelieving smile plays on his lips. "Oh yeah? Doing what?"

I tell him what I want and, for a second, he just stares at me. "Please?" I ask.

"All right," he says finally. I exhale. "But I don't get a break for another hour."

"I'll wait."

Right then, a tall guy with greasy-looking blond hair, wearing a red Heaven's Cycle shirt, comes out from the door behind the counter. "Dude, it's not acceptable to just leave ... Who's this?"

"Dani." I nod at him.

The man throws Spencer a look. "Nice to meet you. Spence is usually too cool to bring his girls around."

"Girls?" I repeat as Spencer rolls his eyes, giving BILL R. a playful shove.

"He's joking."

"So you need a bike?" asks BILL R.

"She's waiting for me."

BILL R. shakes his head. "Oh, no you don't! Dude, don't *even* think you can try to ditch me with all the work we have for the rest of the day."

"I'm not," Spencer says, but BILL R., not appearing to have heard, continues, "I mean, I'm glad you have a girlfriend or whatever, but—"

"She's not"—Spencer glances at me—"my girlfriend."

"You *know* Trey doesn't like us getting visits during work hours."

"I am NOT leaving you," Spencer says.

BILL R. pauses thoughtfully, holding up a hand. "Chill, bro. That's all you had to say to begin with. And thanks, I appreciate you doing your job and cleaning up after your own shit."

"Just ignore him," Spencer tells me as soon as BILL R. disappears out the door. He leans against the counter. "So, what are you gonna do for an hour? Or do you want to go and come back?"

"I'll wait."

Spencer opens his mouth to say something, but right at that moment, BILL R.'s head reappears in the doorway leading into the store's garage. "Just a friendly reminder that the tires will not move themselves." BILL R. smiles at me. "Nice to meet you, Dani."

He vanishes again and, after a momentary pause to ensure that he doesn't return, Spencer says, "Well, I can log you in on the computer if you want to check e-mail or whatever. Play solitaire. I don't really know what you want to do."

"Sounds like a plan," I say, and follow him behind the counter.

"Sit," he tells me.

I slip into the leather computer chair and wait as he leans over me, his long tattooed arms coming down on either side of me. He smells like wood and cigarettes and burned tires. A couple of taps on the keyboard later, he's no longer leaning over me.

"Let me know if you need anything."

"Thanks," I say. He heads into the door BILL R. appeared from. The computer is so slow, it might be older than I am. While waiting for chess to open up, I wonder what I'm supposed to do if the phone rings or if a customer walks in. Probably I'll just act like I work here or totally ignore them. I'm especially good at option 2.

I suck at chess. I'm concentrating so hard on not having the computer annihilate me that I barely notice when someone by the name of HardCoreKandi starts IMing Spencer.

I ignore the IMs at first, but, when I grow tired of losing to the computer, I decide I can afford to volunteer a little brain-power to telling the annoying IMer where to go shove it.

> HardCoreKandi: HEY!!!! So guess who just got IM?
> HardCoreKandi: ME!!!! LOL. Txt is so much easier.
> HardCoreKandi: Spence, are you ignoring me?
> HardCoreKandi: I don't take too kindly to that. LOL.
> SpencersAss: Actually, yes, I was ignoring you.

I'm busy being amused by Spencer's IM name when, all of a sudden, it hits me.

> SpencersAss: Oh my God, it's you! Candy!
> HardCoreKandi: I spell it Kandi, but yeah, it's me. LOL.
> SpencersAss: I like your screen name.
> HardCoreKandi: Really? Thanks. I like yours too. And not just
>   as a screen name. LOL.

An involuntary shudder escapes me. But, of course, there's no way I'm going back to a chess game I was losing now.

> SpencersAss: Yeah, it's really classy. HardCoreKandi. Sounds
>   like the title of something in a Triple X store. Or
>   maybe the stage persona of an exotic dancer.
> HardCoreKandi: LOL, really? The title of something you've
>   seen? LOL.

This girl has so many problems.

HardCoreKandi: I feel like we never really talk at school
anymore. Not like old times :(
SpencersAss: You know what it is, HardCoreKandi?
HardCoreKandi: What? And you don't have to keep calling me
HardCoreKandi. HCK works. LOL.
SpencersAss: Sorry, HCK. Listen, don't take this the wrong
way, okay? But every time I try to have a
conversation with you, I just get distracted.
Your roots are hideous. Blond roots on black
hair just looks wrong.

Five minutes pass before she replies. I've leaned back in my
seat, making myself more comfortable by stretching out my
legs beneath the desk. I've even gone back to playing chess.

HardCoreKandi: Spence, you crack me up. LOL. What are you
doing right now?
SpencersAss: IMing you.
HardCoreKandi: Well obvi. But what else are you doing? I feel
like hanging out.
SpencersAss: What's stopping you?

A minute so she can process.

HardCoreKandi: With you silly. LOL.
SpencersAss: So HKC, what do you have against Danielle
Bailey? I personally think she's hot.

HardCoreKandi: Are you kidding?? And it's H–C–K.

SpencersAss: She doesn't have regrowth.

HardCoreKandi: She's a bitch.

SpencersAss: If I have to hump a dog, I'd rather she were female, thank you.

HardCoreKandi: ??

HardCoreKandi: Don't *ever* talk to me about humping Danielle.

SpencersAss: HKC, this conversation is going nowhere. Let's just agree to disagree . . . Can we talk about the time you wet your pants in third grade?

HardCoreKandi: WTF?

SpencersAss: Oh, you remember.

HardCoreKandi: Actually, NO I DON'T. Stop being such a jerk, Spence.

SpencersAss: See, Dani would have said "stop being such an ass Spencer'sAss." That's another reason I like her—her comic timing.

HardCoreKandi: Stop being an a–hole or I'll leave.

SpencersAss: Does this offer stand lunchtime Monday too?

HardCoreKandi: I don't get it.

HardCoreKandi: :(

SpencersAss: Never mind, HKC. What can I say to get you overkilling those LOLs again?

HardCoreKandi: I told you. Stop being a jerk. Or you could come over with Dunkin Donuts :-)

SpencersAss: Okay, something that doesn't require effort or
              seeing your hair. (Be honest, did you *ever* think
              that perm was a good idea?)
SpencersAss: The first night, maybe?
HardCoreKandi has signed out of this conversation.

I spend the next ten minutes finishing up my chess game. Predictably, I lose.

"You still here?" Spencer walks toward me, wiping his hands on a yellow cloth and then throwing it down on the counter. "Ready?"

"Yep." I stand and follow him out of the store and back around it. "There's a slight chance your relationship with Candace has been irreparably damaged."

He frowns, his forehead creasing. "A slight chance? What did you do?"

I give him a quick rundown as we approach his motorcycle. A well-oiled, shiny black machine. Also, the favor I've requested.

"Here." He hands me a helmet and climbs on. When I make no move to get on, he turns back. "What's wrong?"

"I thought you were going to let me drive."

"Your first go?" He shakes his head. "Hell no."

"But I've driven before." The fact that Spencer is so worldly makes it difficult to lie to him. Harder than it usually is. I bite the inside of my cheek as I wait for his response. This is important.

"Okay," he sighs, "but I'll ride behind you."

He gets off and I get on. Then he gives me a long lecture

and explanation of what everything does. Afterward, he quizzes me on everything he's said. For some reason, I want to burst out laughing. Spencer doesn't exactly strike me as the explaining, teaching kind. But the crazy things we do for the things we love. In this case, his bike.

"I swear, if this thing gets a single scratch," he warns as he fixes his helmet. I start the motorcycle and we take off, at snail's speed at first. It's a good thing I'm a fast learner.

His arms wrap tightly around my waist and, instead of holding on for dear life, like I might have been if I was sitting in the back and he was driving, he seems to be pulling me down, keeping me from crashing into the bike and into the strong wind that blows against us.

Ten minutes later, we're in the park and Spencer makes us stop. "You did really well," he says in a tone that would sound encouraging coming from someone who encourages, but just sounds patronizing from him. Even though we're at a full stop, his arms are still around my waist. I think he likes them there.

"Wanna get off?" I whisper.

"Sure."

He gets off the bike and starts to take off his helmet. I unbuckle mine, hand it to him, but don't get off.

Spencer is fast.

So fast that when I restart his motorcycle and drive forward, twisting the grip to accelerate, I'm afraid he's going to catch up with me.

Except he doesn't.

His yells and—I'm sorry—his shrieks are lost in the swishing of the wind, along with his frantic footsteps.

I drive fast, really fast, so fast that it happens before I have time to reconsider.

One second he's behind me, sprinting to stop me from hurting his motorcycle. The next, he's right above me, yelling, still yelling.

I panic.

This had to have done it.

How can it not have worked? I'm so angry that I can't breathe; so frustrated, I can't swallow.

But then I taste it. The smell and flavor of iron. Blood.

As if to confirm it, my head tingles, my muscles—well, I can't feel them, but they don't seem okay either.

"Oh my God!" Spencer screams. And this time, I know he's not yelling about his motorcycle and the fact that I ran it into the biggest tree in this park. He's speaking now, frantically, but the words hover around me, falling and dripping with blood. I think he's on the phone, calling somebody.

Or maybe not, because he keeps talking to me.

"Why didn't you stop, Dani?" he yells. "Why the hell didn't you stop? Oh *shit*, Dani. *Shit*."

I feel bad. I do.

But mostly, I feel dead.

I like that feeling.

five

14

Jena and I are taking a walk to the cafeteria. Are you sure you don't need anything?" my father asks me, standing in the doorway of the hospital examination room. It's funny; Jena is the one whose body can't fight anything, and yet here she sits beside my bed with my mother and my father, making sure I am still alive.

"I'm sure." Mom's gaze is focused on mine as Jena rises from her position on the chair next to my bed. I know Mom is making a concerted effort not to look at her, because then she might change her mind and have to focus on her instead. Even though I'm lying here half-naked in one of those spotted cotton hospital gowns, it's obvious who's sick and who isn't. Sure, I'm covered in scrapes; I have three stitches above my right eye and more on my thigh and a wrist that might be broken. But you almost need a microscope to find Jena. Her bones and veins are bigger than her. Bluish, greenish, reddish lines that run across her body, rebelliously tattooed all over her, claiming her. I bet that's what my mother does when she sneaks into Jena's room in the mornings. She's replicating the colors on herself, so the cancer voodoo gods know where to send it. The red right here, the green right there, the blue everywhere. Everywhere a blue-blue.

I watch Jena as she disappears out the door behind Dad. She's feeling better than she was this morning, still weak, but well enough to go home today. Does that mean it worked? Did *my* life make her better?

"We need to talk, Danielle." Mom crosses her arms in front of her chest.

"I know." I nod, then wince from the pain. "Let me guess, Brad and Jen are back together. Or Walmart is bankrupt."

She stares at me, her face tight and pinched, wrinkles gathering on her forehead, the side of her eyes, and just above her upper lip.

"I'm serious, Danielle." Two Danielles in a row.

I decide to play it safe and bite my tongue—she *does* look serious. I lean back against the pillow and wait for her to speak.

"I got in touch with Brody Richardson—my friend? He said he'd pull some strings to get you into another round of callbacks two weeks from today."

I stare at her. That's not what she wants to say and we both know it.

"So I guess I shouldn't have tried to ride—" I start to say at the same time as she says, talking well above me, "From now on, some things are going to change around here."

"It was an accident."

Her eyes won't meet mine, but I can tell by the crease between her eyebrows that she doesn't believe me.

"You're not invincible, Dani." I hate it when her voice cracks.

I open my mouth to speak. How much does she know? How much is either of us willing to say?

I shut my mouth and stare at my hands in my lap.

She brushes some invisible lint off the edge of my bed. "You are going to start seeing Dr. Livingstone. She's a well-respected therapist I—"

"A *shrink*?" Despite the shooting pain up my neck, I sit up. "I told you it was an—"

"Sit down," Mom orders. I lean back obediently. "And that's just one of the changes.

"I don't know what you could possibly be thinking, Danielle," she is saying now, her eyes still trained on the bed. I'm surprised at how strong and determined her voice is. "With everything that is going on with Jena, do you really expect us to be chasing after you, too? You know that's not fair."

"I'm sorry," I say, but she's not done.

"This is hard on every single one of us. I don't even . . . I don't feel like a person most days. A shadow of a person, maybe, stumbling around and trying to make sense of everything."

"I'll be more careful."

She doesn't say anything for a second and all I hear is the sound of her plucking loose threads from the sheets. Maybe she thinks if she pulls hard enough it will all unravel and she can start again and make something better, something that doesn't fall apart.

"You have no idea how angry I am with you right now. You could have . . . seriously injured yourself."

You could have died.

Except I couldn't. Not for real, not yet. *Is she keeping track?* I wonder. "I'm sorry."

Again, she doesn't seem to hear me. "This is the last thing we need right now, Danielle. The very last thing. Your sister needs us. She needs all of us to be here for her."

Nobody ever talks about the other side, the part where we need *her*. Instead we get to stand up and grow up and stop putting on makeup and *be strong* for Jena, while she gets to lie there and become weakness, let it eat at her, nibble at her toenails and overpower her.

I don't say anything. I'm biting the inside of my cheek and it's starting to bleed.

"Do you understand what I'm saying?"

"I'm sorry."

"Stop saying that," she says finally. "Just show me. Show us."

I nod.

Dad pops his head in to say the two of them are going home. Jena Baby is sleepy. All she wants is to lie down and melt into her bed.

We're waiting on an X-ray of my wrist, so I can't leave yet.

"Go ahead without me," Mom says. He leaves and it's just the two of us again, plus an obnoxious Silence that takes up the whole room, forcing us to shut up just so he can hear himself talk.

"Are you in pain?" Mom asks after a minute, jolting me from my thoughts.

"No," I lie, "why?"

She finds where it hurts anyway. My temples and the right side of my jaw. Her fingers draw little circles around them, trying to erase both the cuts she can see and the ones she can't. It's then it occurs to me to tell her. About the cats and catching lives. About the moment when I was drowning and everything started to make sense. About why and where and when it all started. It's easiest to point to the accident, to the things my mother whispered, but I don't know where to start. And I wouldn't know where to end.

So I sit silently as she gently massages my head, no words passing between us.

Four lives down, five to go.

It's six-thirty in the evening when we get home, but I might as well have stayed in the hospital given the reception I get at home. Jena is furious with me and communicates this by not communicating with me at all. After hours of silent treatment, though, she storms into my room in the middle of the night, blinding me by flooding the room with light. "I wouldn't ever forgive you. You should know that."

Naturally, the one time I actually fall asleep at a decent hour, I am rudely awakened. I grunt in response.

"You mysteriously fall into the pool, then you mysteriously wind up in a motorcycle accident. What are you *doing*, Dani?" she asks, but I can hear from her voice that she has some ideas.

Jena is not magically well, but she was well enough not to have to stay overnight at the hospital; she's better than she was this morning. Is this it? Does she get slightly better with each life I lose?

Or do I just need to lose the *right* one to make her completely well? I imagine one of my lives wriggling out from beneath my ribs, floating around until it settles somewhere safe and cancer-free inside her. Maybe it fills the hollow space inside her bones, where the marrow goes.

Jena sits at the foot of my bed. "Mom says she doesn't believe in accidents."

"Tell her congrats," because what else am I supposed to say?

"She says there's a reason for everything and I started thinking . . ." Her voice is soft, contemplative. "Why do you think there's two of us? If there are no coincidences."

When I don't answer, she says, "What if we're each other's backups? I'm here in case something happens to you, and you're here in case something happens to me. I mean, that makes sense, right? That we're each other's backups?"

I nod, but if it's true, I'm a useless backup. I can't help Jena because I'm not her match; I don't know if I'm helping her now, if the lives I've lost have really paid off.

She leans back on the foot of my bed, and neither of us speaks.

How is it possible that I miss her when she's right here?

She's beside me, but I am hearing her move about in her room down the hall; she's singing along to a rock song. Then we are on the couch downstairs, fighting over what to watch on TV or get for takeout, arguing about who finished the shampoo without telling Mom we were out. We are running in wild circles around the park near our house. We are seven again, blurry gray figures chasing after each other.

I will go on existing without her. Wear dresses she has never seen. One birthday cake instead of two.

The thought is so absurd that I almost burst out laughing.

I don't remember falling asleep, but when I wake up about an hour later, she is curled up at the foot of my bed, breathing in and breathing out.

I know I should wake her, or move her to her room before Mom gets up, but I like having her here. I go back to sleep.

I miss the whole week of school against my will. Not so much because of my injuries; my parents are scared to let me out of their sight. They lock me up and chain me to my sister on her couch, in front of her game shows with the cheesy hosts and disturbingly overenthusiastic contestants, to ensure that both daughters live to greet tomorrow.

Today my mother pulls back her hair in a tight ponytail that looks like it has to hurt. She goes between the two of us making cups of hot chocolate and rewrapping wounds and fractured wrists, offering to move pillows and trying to make us talk, to each other, but mostly to her. When that doesn't work, she mentions something about a new recipe she's been wanting to try and retires to the kitchen, where she only has to remember she has one sick daughter and she can pretend the other one is at school.

An hour passes before Mom returns. She tells me she just got off the phone with Dr. Livingstone, her child psychologist friend. My mother knows important people, you see.

She takes Jena's temperature and force-feeds her medicine and suddenly *The Price Is Right* is interesting. I can't tear my eyes away from Bob Barker and the woman with the vertical eyebrows. (It's not something I want to get into.) Then we have lunch and I heap praises upon Mom's mushroom and tofu soup, even though I keep throwing up in my mouth. Mom beams, so I continue, "God, Mom, maybe you should go on one of those cooking shows on TV. I bet you could win."

And Mom beams some more, and I keep massaging her cooking ego so she doesn't notice that I'm not eating, but maybe I've gone too far, because Jena can't stop laughing.

For a while, we just ignore her. Until she starts to snort-laugh and her shoulders are shaking, and me and Mom both notice because we're afraid her head might fall off. Her head that is bigger than her shoulders.

But she just keeps laughing and, all of a sudden, I'm laughing, too.

Mom doesn't get it. She looks between the two of us, a

mixture of hurt and confusion on her face. "What's so funny, you two?"

And we laugh even harder because she doesn't get it, so she just smiles and fake-laughs so she feels like she's in on the joke. I feel bad for her and I want to explain, but when Jena laughs, everyone laughs. It's a rule.

I don't know who stops laughing first. We still have to eat. I wonder if the Mom and Jena days, the ones where I'm not home and they hang out together and are mother-and-daughter-best-friends—I wonder if they're this good.

15

When my mother said change, she meant God. Or, at least, she meant church.

I'd hoped she would have forgotten after a week, but apparently not.

Jena's on Mom's left. Cushioned between Mom and my father—he's even wearing a tie—I slump in my seat and people-watch.

There's a preppy girl with long blond hair who has a tall, dark-haired guy draped around her for, I'm guessing, decorative purposes. There's no way she's as into him as he is into her, but maybe she is, and she just can't show it because they're in church. They're sitting directly in front of me.

There's also the pastor, who might be fairly fascinating if I wasn't trying so hard to tune him out. I mean, I think that's a tattoo on his wrist. But I have to stop looking at him.

There's a group of old people sitting close to the front, with a tall woman in floral scrubs at the edge of one row, casting occasional glances at them. I think she's a nurse, here to make sure if one of them falls, she can convince all the others to propagate the whole "your grandmother died peacefully in her sleep" lie.

My grandmother lived with us for the last six weeks of her life. The night she died, she didn't mutter about bright lights or singing angels or anything like that. Probably she didn't even go to heaven. Jena and I struggled to fall asleep as she hacked and groaned and yelped at my mother and her nurse and anyone that came within six feet of her. I don't know what it is about parents, but they always think the worlds they build for you are soundproof. The next morning, they tearfully broke the news to us: *Grandma went to heaven early this morning. She went peacefully in her sleep.* We nodded and pretended we didn't know the truth about old people and how they die. But we did.

"Stop that," Mom whispers. For a second, I think she's talking to me. Then I realize she's actually scolding my dad, who keeps fidgeting with the bulletin they handed us when we came in, clamping and unclamping his sweaty hands.

At the end of the service, we're bombarded by more people than I'd like. Apparently, Mom really has recruited a whole army of people to pray for Jena.

"I feel claustrophobic," Jena whispers to me, after a woman releases her from a minute-long embrace. So I stay put on her right side and square my shoulders bodyguard-style, which makes Jena giggle. "God, you're an embarrassment."

But clearly something about me screams beefy martial arts specialist because, for the most part, the space invasions devolve into hearty shoulder squeezes and back pats.

"You must be Danielle!" a lady says suddenly, taking my hands in hers, even though it's a little awkward since my left arm is in a cast. "You look just like your mother."

I mumble a response even I'm not sure of, while behind me an elderly man speaks to Jena.

"I've been praying for you," the lady says, still squeezing my hands.

Mom appears beside me then and thanks her, as I try to keep my expression even. Why is she praying for *me*, and not Jena? All I have are some measly bruises and a crack in my wrist. Maybe girls with nine lives have prebooked tickets to hell.

As soon as I get my hands back, I scoot to the edge of the group and stay off to the side so Mom can do all the talking. Dad seems to have taken over my duties as Jena's buffer.

Thankfully, Jena is ready to go home and informs Mom, who begins to speed-talk.

Meanwhile, the three of us excuse ourselves and start toward the car. We're barely in when Dad begins to loosen his tie.

"I need a smoke," he mutters to himself. Then, hurriedly, he looks back at the two of us. "I didn't mean . . ."

"It's okay, Dad. We all need a smoke," I reassure him.

Dad hasn't smoked, as far as anyone knows, in about a year, and the way Mom sees it, that's One Big Disease conquered this year.

A couple of seconds later, Mom climbs into the car and he goes back to being on good behavior.

The rest of the way home, Mom and Dad discuss, with

entirely too much enthusiasm, what other changes we're going to implement. They mention family outings and visiting extended family.

Drawing on inspiration from the service, I pray vehemently that neither of these things comes to pass.

When I get to school on Monday, everybody is huddled in corners, whispering and snickering and passing secret-code glances. Which reminds me of my cast and the fact that it's making its school debut. It's not like I'm hiding a sorry case of leprosy under the cast, but I still feel a little self-conscious.

By eavesdropping on Jen Mullins and Karen Li's conversation while "retrieving stuff from my locker," I learn that I am not entertaining enough to feed the rumor mill after all. They are gossiping about Lauren getting suspended. *Lauren. Suspended.* Apparently, without the influence of my good character, Rachel Talbot convinced her to break into the teacher's lounge over the weekend, unscrew all the lightbulbs in there, and scribble a message on the wall, in permanent marker, that said, *You steal our rights, we steal your lights.*

The whole story is so bizarre, I don't even talk to Jack in math, except to agree to meet in the library at lunch to work on our project.

"What happened to your arm?" he asks, glancing up from the book he is reading when I sit beside him at a table in the library.

"I broke my wrist," I inform him, sliding into the chair

across from him and flipping over the *National Geographic* magazine left on the table. Educational magazines strategically placed *right at the fingertips of students* is a ploy devised by Mrs. Uri to lure kids into excellence. Unconcerned about giving her false hope, I open it and idly flip through the pages.

"How?" Jack asks, staring at me. His piercing look makes me feel uncomfortable and I glance back down at the page.

"I had an accident." I snap the magazine shut and lean forward across the table. "Listen, thanks for your concern, sweet thang, but I think we should focus on the task ahead. This project is really important to me."

He glances down. "Don't call me . . . that."

"What, hot stuff?" I bat my eyelashes and inch forward just a little more.

"How did you break it?"

I sigh. I don't understand why we're still taking about this. "I was in a motorcycle accident. So about the assignment . . ." I slide the papers in front of him toward myself.

"Dani?"

"Hmm."

"Are you sure you're okay?"

I leaf through the pages. "You know, I think I liked my information better."

Undeterred, Jack continues, "Because you don't really . . . I mean you seemed upset that day outside. After the chips thing? And actually, since school started you've been . . . different."

"Listen, Jack," I snap finally. "I really appreciate your . . .

well, whatever . . . but from the start of this project, I think I've made it abundantly clear—despite your many advances—that we should have a strictly platonic relationship and just focus on getting our work done."

"Platonic? You call me . . . *names*"—he flushes—"all the time." God, he's still talking.

"Out of friendship," I say.

"You're flirting with me."

I laugh, and it comes out slightly more bitter than even I expect. "Seriously? You think that's *flirting*? It's called bullying, Jack. I'm being a bitch." Because I am a bitch. Look what I did to Spencer and his bike. And to Mom, and to Dad, and Jena.

Jack doesn't say anything. And maybe it's because we went to church or whatever, but suddenly I'm fighting this urge to apologize. It would be utterly lame. Since when do I care about Jack or anyone else's feelings?

"So, this sucks." I push the paper toward him, but he completely ignores me, staring down at the book he's reading.

When zero words and fifteen minutes have passed, I decide Jack and I would probably benefit from a little distance. I think about going to find Lauren, before it hits me that she's not at school. She's *suspended*. I locate a corner at the back of the library, where I pull out a book on cats and start reading. It talks about litters and their diet and behaviors. It doesn't mention any of the important things, though. Nothing about transferring lives from one cat to another.

"Jena used to sit behind me in Spanish class," Jack blurts

out from above me, sounding more like he's letting out his breath after holding it for a long time. "I mean, we never really talked or anything, but she sat behind me."

My voice is emotionless, flat. "She's not dead." Not flat enough. And I hate past tense.

"I know," Jack says, sitting down next to me. I start to point out that a) I didn't invite him to, and b) his pants length is too short and if I see his socks, I *will* act out, but it's too late. He's right next to me. "I don't think she's going to die."

My stomach knots. Why are we talking about this? "You don't know."

"Do you?"

"Nobody knows," I mutter, because I want to have the last word and because who the hell is Jack Penner?

I don't want to talk about Jena. Not with him, not with her, not with anyone. Not even with me.

16

I want to die eating peanut M&M's.

I've only just figured this out.

"See, the thing for me is that I always want filling. Chocolate by itself is just, well, *plain*," I explain.

My child psychologist nods sympathetically, running her tongue over her teeth to gather bits of chocolate. It would be hard to maintain the whole I'm-going-to-figure-out-all-your-child's-issues-and-give-you-a-new-model-with-extended-warranty image if her teeth looked like a chocolate slug had slithered all over them. Conveniently for me, though, it's just an image. My parents managed to snag the only shrink within a fifty-thousand-mile radius willing to facilitate discussion on candy for a hundred bucks an hour.

"Peanut butter," Harriet call-me-Harry-with-an-*i* Livingstone says, "is glorified, liquefied peanut. So how can you like peanut M&M's and not peanut butter M&M's?"

"Texture," I say instantly, folding my legs beneath me and digging through the bowl of candy Harry-with-an-*i* handed me when I walked in. Apparently, she buys different types of M&M's and mixes them together into the same bag to create her own rainbow-colored M&M concoction—an excellent quality in any mental health professional, if you ask me.

Harry-with-an-*i* is a forty-something-year-old former beauty queen turned Serious Child Psychologist that my mother knew from college. She isn't much taller than me, but wears three-inch pumps, a purple business suit (feminine but Serious) and has a dark spot in the cleft of her chin.

I'm cautiously weeding out the M&M's, being careful to leave the peanut butter and plain ones. I have this theory that the peanut ones look a little pregnant, a little rounder around the middle, some stretch marks on the candy coating. So far, it's been foolproof.

Harry-with-an-*i* stands and reaches for the clipboard on the table now. If I were paying better attention, I might make something of it.

"When I was growing up," she begins in a slow, formal voice, "my whole life changed in one night. My uncle's truck rolled off a highway one winter evening and it took nearly all night to find him. They found him in the river just out of town. I was about your age."

Red. Green.

"That sucks," I say. "At least it wasn't gory. He just drowned, didn't he?"

Harry-with-an-*i* clicks her Parker pen on, itching to start taking notes. "He didn't die, Danielle. We found him alive. And drowning, or any kind of death, is gory."

Orange. Brown. Orange.

It feels like she's waiting.

"Oh. Well, all's well that ends well, then."

She shifts in her white leather couch. If my mom were here, she'd tell her how impractical white furniture is. "The whole thing was hugely significant for me. I ended up being terrified of driving. So much so that I didn't learn to drive till I was twenty-five. I think my fear in many ways pushed me into this profession." Her voice softens. "I empathize with people who are afraid. I've been there."

Green. Blue. Orange. Red.

"I remember being worried that people wouldn't get it if I explained why I was so afraid. I never saw the accident myself. I certainly wasn't *in* it. But none of that mattered. It was still traumatizing."

Orange. Yellow. Brown. I wonder if this is her default story. The one she goes to right after she breaks out the bowl of M&M's and sugar-sedates her patients so they confess all kinds of things to her and convince themselves they're scared of driving, too.

Green. Orange. Brown. Blue.

"What are you afraid of, Danielle?"

I struggle to think. The right answer: "Driving."

Harry-with-an-*i* laughs even though it's not funny and

neither of us is joking and I'm starting to be over this and I think she knows.

"Okay, good answer. What else?"

"Santa," I say, "creeps me out. I mean, he just strikes me as a little, you know, weird. Breaking into chimneys, drinking your milk and cookies."

Harry-with-an-*i* is staring at me, sort of listlessly, like maybe she doesn't know where to go now or she's thinking this is the easiest hundred dollars she's earned.

I lean back and fold my arms across my chest, then quickly unfold them to save a lone yellow M&M before it slides into the side of the couch. It's not so much that I care about protecting her furniture from the melted brown chocolate; it's more that I want to eat it. Plus, it's especially pregnant, which means there has to be a giant peanut baby in there.

I can feel Harry-with-an-*i* watching me, so I offer her some M&Ms.

"No thanks," she shakes her head. "I shouldn't have any more."

Then, evidently deciding to go another route—and not terribly optimistic about it, if her expression is anything to go by—Harry-with-an-*i* holds her pen to the page and says, "Dani, tell me about Jena. And how you're dealing with the situation."

Green—peanut.

"Well," I say, chewing, "to be honest, I'm not doing so well."

"Really?" Her pen lightly scratches the page and I can tell

this is what she considers success. A sentence or two that summarize me, a paragraph to decipher me.

"Yeah. Like, for instance, the other day, I had this really massive headache."

She glances up.

"Oh, and then a few weeks ago, I had a runny nose. I sneezed a couple of times today in gym class, too."

The pen doesn't move, although it wants to.

"Danielle. I mean how do you feel *emotionally*. Mentally. Spiritually. Not physically."

Orange—peanut.

Blue—peanut.

Red—two peanuts.

"Listen," she says. "I know the last thing you want is to have to sit in a room with some stranger and discuss something that is so hard to talk about. But I also want you to know that I'm here to help. Whatever you say will just be between the two of us."

"Good. I was worried you'd tell my dad what I said about Santa. We haven't told him we know about his nonexistence yet. Or that, in general, Santa sucks."

Harry-with-an-*i* shakes her head and chuckles lightly. "You have quite a sense of humor, you know that?"

"I was being serious."

She puts down her pad. "I'll give you the entire bag of M&M's in my drawer if you'll give me one sentence. Just one sentence about how you honestly feel."

"How big is the bag?"

She stands up, goes around the desk, and pulls it out. It's reasonable, probably weighs about ten pounds, since it contains all the different kinds of M&M's she's mixed together.

This is bribery, I want to say. Instead, I stick a brown M&M in my mouth. "Can I say it now?" Peanut butter. It floods my mouth and my saliva drowns in it and I just want to spit it out all over her sterile, hip-psychologist office.

"The sentence? Of course! Go ahead." I start to open my mouth, but she stops me again. "Remember. I want honest and I want it to relate to the Jena situation."

"I feel," I say, feeling myself choke on the peanut butter M&M, "like that bag is the size of my sister."

She stares at me for a second, down at the bag on her desk, and then back up at me. She looks at me for so long, her eyes boring into me, like she has X-ray vision, and I want to go home but not home to them and her and me but somewhere else. Just when I think that was not the right sentence and she will surely want more—maybe an office-full of peanut-butter-flavored barf, since that's the best I can do right now—she pushes the bag across her desk. "When your father picks you up, ask him to help you carry it out."

There are exactly three minutes left of our session and she sits behind her desk, writing on her clipboard, and lets me eat my M&M's.

Except I don't eat them.

I let them roll off my lap when Harry-with-an-*i* isn't

looking. Into the spaces between the couch, empty spaces of nothing and darkness, and I help the ones that miss. When all M&M's are comfortably accommodated and hidden, I point out that it's the end of our time together, pick up the bag from her desk, and haul it out into the waiting room, which would be a lot easier if I could use two hands instead of one.

Dad shows up late, looking tired and tentative, but hopeful. Probably he's wondering if I'm cured. I tell him Harry-with-an-*i* let me have the giant M&M bag. He helps me put it in the trunk of the car (since there are certain things tofu-obsessed mothers can live without knowing), but he doesn't ask about it.

17

For the past few months, evenings have revolved around preparations for chemo or radiation or one of Jena's appointments the next day, but tonight I am sitting on the edge of the bathtub in my parents' bathroom, as Mom leans over me, giving me bangs to cover the stitches on my forehead for callbacks this weekend.

I sit quietly and watch pieces of my hair twirl to the ground. Mom squints and frowns and trims. When she is done, I'm disappointed at how much I still look like myself. How much hair do you need to start with, to cut and cut and keep recognizing yourself? How much hair do you have to lose to become unrecognizable?

I don't even notice, until Jena points it out, that the bangs are slightly uneven.

On Wednesday when I walk into the cafeteria, the smell of B.O. and mystery meat thick in the air, I can't shake the feeling that I've just lost another friend. Since I crashed his motorcycle,

Spencer hasn't said one word to me. He didn't even come to the hospital after. I would sit with Lauren again, but it's her first day back post-suspension and she stayed in to catch up on Spanish. So I walk toward Spencer and Candy's table.

The sparkle in Candy's eyes, her confidence and the fact that she actually *brightens* to see me approaching, only reinforces my feeling of unease. "Oh, hi, Danielle. We were just talking about you."

I drop my tray beside Spencer, whose head is straight down, seemingly extra-attentive to his food.

"Funny, because everyone's talking about that nose piercing you got." And the accompanying infection.

She perks ups. "Really?"

"I haven't seen you in forever," I tell Spencer, who still hasn't looked at me.

Candy butts in. "Actually, that's just what we were talking about." Her voice is high-pitched and so ecstatic she seems to be tripping over her words. "Spencer and I *love* you. We do."

"Not as much as I love you, Spencer. And you too, what is it, *Hard Candy Core*?"

She narrows her eyes at me, all out of sweetness. "We no longer want you to sit with us. Poor Spencer has enough crap on his plate without you going and crashing his motorcycle."

"Does *poor Spencer* have so much crap on his plate that he can't tell me himself?" I'm looking at him, not her. He's still looking at his burger.

"I've been in trouble before," he mumbles. "The last thing

I needed was to spend an hour getting questioned by the police. And I could have been fired."

"It was an accident," I say, forgetting for a minute not to care.

"Well." Candy claps her hands. "We're lucky the cops saw it that way and that we were able to avoid a potentially nasty situation. I'm glad we all agree that the best thing is to go our separate ways." She draws the imaginary separating line with her and Spencer on one side, and me on the other. "Spencey and I knew you'd understand."

Even he reacts to that one. "Don't effing call me that."

"Sorry," she says quickly, and I realize that they, Spandy or Canspence, are going to self-destruct. She's too eager to please, too desperate to prove herself, and Spencer is kind of an asshead.

I go from the cafeteria to the bathroom, lock myself in a stall, and wait for lunchtime to pass. Sadly, time slows down, moving at sixty-one seconds a minute and sixty-one minutes an hour, so that being trapped in a five-inch-by-five-inch space quickly loses its novelty. I claw my way out and head down the hall again, stopping at the empty classroom where we usually have math. The wise thing would be for me to start in on the mountain of homework that was sent home—and which I managed to ignore—when I missed school last week.

Instead, I shuffle to a desk at the back and rest my head on it.

I'm starting to doze when I hear footsteps, and then in walks Halbrook, his face stuck between the covers of a book.

He's startled when he notices me. "Oh, hi, Danielle. I didn't see you there." His book is *War and Peace* and I half-wonder if

he'll decide to read aloud to us next class, instead of us working on our assignments.

"Are you all right?"

I'm surprised he hasn't gone back to his reading yet. "Perfect."

"How's your sister doing?"

Halbrook hates Jena. She used to forge notes all the time for
fake track meets and sporting events. That's not why he hates
her, though. I think it has to do with the fact that she once
did it for every student in his math class. It was only a joke, of
course, but Halbrook isn't exactly known for his sense of humor.

My parents gave her the third degree when they learned of
her activities. If she did something like that now, they'd be secretly delighted. We're all searching for signs the old Jena still
exists.

"Perfect, too," I mutter, feeling the desk beginning to im-
print itself on my cheek.

"And how's your project coming?"

Here's a question for him: Why is he expressing teacherly
concern over me instead of reading *War and Freaking Peace*?

"You'll be blown away," I tell him, though Jack and I got
next to nothing done during lunch on Monday.

When he leaves the classroom again, I close my eyes and
try to fall asleep. I dream Mr. Halbrook hovers over me, halo
made of concern as his book sits unattended at his desk. I
dream he and the rest of the world hesitate around me, pray
for me and try to help, and yet I don't let them.

I wake up with a self-prescribed mandate for normalcy. Tomorrow, I will catch up on all the work I've missed. Tomorrow, I will bring my T. rex–sized bag of M&M's and share with all my classmates, let them sift through the round nuggets of deception, trying to sort good from evil, peanut from peanut butter. Peanut butter is a wolf in peanut's clothing. Shame on it.

Focus, Dani.

Tomorrow, when I return to popularity and humanity and *normalcy*, I will not give people any more reasons to wonder.

Lots of people have sisters with cancer. Lots and lots of people. Some people have buried their sisters and brothers and mothers and fathers and aunts and uncles, and I have not.

Some people have sat by their loved ones and watched them hack or hurt or throw up early, too early in the morning, so often that they can no longer fall asleep, and so, they now draw all over themselves and do strange voodoo, and I have not.

Some people have gotten cancer and had to quit school and stay home to Be Sick, a full-time calling, but one that is thoroughly wrong for them since they are the strong ones and they win state soccer championships and so they can't have cancer, and I have not.

I should be grateful, ecstatic.

Many people have died from car crashes, from infections, from drowning, from motorcycles, and I have not.

I keep waking up.

18

Saturday morning brings my father standing over me, nudging me awake. Today is the makeup callback.

I tell him I'd rather stay in bed and let it swallow me whole. He laughs and squeezes my shoulder. "Come on, sleepyhead."

Still asleep, I trudge into the bathroom and splash cold water on my face. We use Colgate, not Whitaden, around here. Since I don't want things to be awkward at the callback, I decide to forgo toothpaste and brushing entirely.

Thanks to the bangs, the only visible reminder of the accident is the cast around my left arm. Mom spoke to Brody Richardson about my most unfortunate accident, and since they won't actually be filming the commercial for another two months, they're willing to overlook the broken wrist.

I walk all the way across the hall. The door to Jena's room is wide open, the torn pieces of paper still hanging limply there, skulls without bones and wordless warning signs.

When I go in, there is no movement, no sound. Even though the door is open, her room is too warm, smells like sweat and dirty laundry. I see a lump in her bed.

Finally, she turns from the wall to face me and I hear myself breathing again. "Where are you going?" she asks.

I can only see her face; the rest is blanket.

"The callback."

"Good luck," she says. I nod, holding on to the doorknob. I mean to pull it toward me to shut the door, but I'm frozen.

Something is wrong.

"See you when you get back," she says. I know that's supposed to tell me she's okay.

I shut the door.

"Hey, there you are!" Dad calls from the foot of the stairs. "I made you some coffee."

"Coffee stains teeth," I say. "You're trying to sabotage me, aren't you?"

Dad laughs, winking at me. "Don't tell your mother." I take the mug from him, bringing it to my lips.

"Where is she?" I ask. "Mom, I mean."

He glances up the stairs. "Asleep. You ready?"

My fingers tingle and my heart sneezes. Dad acts appropriately enthusiastic as we walk to the garage and get into the car, but I still can't shake the feeling that something isn't right. It's nine a.m. on Saturday. The only way Mom is sleeping is if she's sedated.

But maybe she is.

I fold myself into the car and try to shut off the crappy brain stuff—the fear, the thoughts. I delete all of it.

Dad doesn't try to make conversation. He presses play on the CD in the car, a *Phantom of the Opera* soundtrack, which my mother had to have left in there. His fingers drum on the steering wheel as he stares out of the glass, far into a darkness I can't see.

"Is something wrong?" I ask.

"There's nothing to worry about." He gives me a tired smile. "I promise. Coffee makes me fidgety."

I don't believe it's just the coffee. "If they're planning to put her down while I'm gone . . ."

"What?" Dad frowns. "Dani, you can't talk . . . You can't say stuff like that. People will take it the wrong way."

"Which people?"

"No, nothing . . . Everything is fine. Would I lie to you?"

Yes. Grandma died peacefully in her sleep.

"Listen, Dans, you have to start trusting people. It's not you against the world, it's *us* against the world. And I'm telling you—today, we're covered."

Silence.

"First, don't ever call me Dans again. Second, I have no idea what you're talking about."

"Sure you do," he says. "You know exactly what I'm talking about. Let's focus on booking this commercial and giving your mom and sister some good news tonight, okay?"

I don't answer.

"Okay?"

I fiddle with the radio. All this wailing is giving me a headache. And not the kind that kills you, so what's the point?

"Okay?"

A pop song fills the car.

"Okay?"

"Dad. For crap's sake."

"O-kay?" he repeats, obnoxiously.

"Whatever." As his mouth opens again, I rush on. "I mean, fine. Sure. Let's do this shit."

"Danielle!"

The next five minutes are devoted to the in-car equivalent of me washing my mouth with soap. I try to point out that a) I've heard Dad curse before, and b) Mom isn't here. So most likely, God isn't either.

"I'm not quite sure that's how it works."

"How *does* it work?" My eyes widen and I turn to face him, attentive and questioning.

He coughs. "Well, you know your mother's the religious one, but I think God is . . . everywhere."

"Really?" If my eyes get any wider, they'll fall out of my head. "Even in the shower and bathroom? Because that's kind of creepy."

"Well . . ."

"And if He's everywhere, why doesn't He stop bad things from happening?"

Dad sighs. "I don't know, Danielle. What do you think?"

I think I'm starting to feel sorry for him. I lean back in my seat. "It doesn't matter. What I think doesn't affect His existence or nonexistence. He either does or doesn't."

He turns to look at me. "That's a good answer. Got any more of those?" His eyes travel back to the road and I get the sense again that today is about more than a toothpaste commercial, and maybe Dad is using me as a buffer between him and the world. By the time we reach our destination, I'm slightly concerned about my breath situation. It's a delicate mix of morning and coffee breath, with bias toward the former.

There are only two of us auditioning today—a blond girl with glistening white teeth. Every time she smiles, it transforms her face, but she doesn't do so often. I wonder who's dying in her family.

At first, I'm there just because I have to be. The first time I read lines, I sort of mumble them, barely trying to conceal my coffee-stained teeth and my irreverent apathy. But then I make the mistake of glancing up at my father, sitting with his hand propped under his chin, watching me.

I thought I'd killed my conscience by now, but she shows up anyway.

If I actually got this part, it would make what has been a universally crappy year for my parents, and Jena, slightly better.

I jerk my chin up and attempt to project horizontally. To say my lines so these people can actually hear them.

My plastic smile falters more than once, but the one on my father's face holds it there. He was proud when I was sort-of-mumbling, practically sleeping up here, shaming his name and taking advantage of his goodness and his need to please Mom. He is still proud.

I am decent in my second-last take, try to go one better for the last, and then I'm done.

Still smiling, I excuse myself and find the nearest bathroom. What was supposed to be a few minutes of (mainly) self-congratulations takes a sharp turn.

My chest starts to hurt. I pull down the cover and collapse on the toilet seat.

I think, *I am on five lives and that's too much.* But that's not it.

My palms sweat, my fingers shake, my eyes well up.

I don't know why and I can't stop it and I hate that I'm sitting on a public toilet doing this and is God here watching creepily or am I alone and make it stop.

It doesn't.

And then I realize what it is.

I just know. Like the time Jena wandered off during our family hiking trip when we were nine. Though I couldn't explain it, I'd just known she was by the lake, and that was where we found her. A twin thing, I suppose.

I run from the bathroom and find my father, who is making some pleasant conversation with a suit. I want to say, "It's too late for flirting, even with a deceptively well-dressed cameraman. And FYI, I said to go for stage moms. Nothing about cameramen."

I don't say that.

Dad starts to introduce the man. "Dani, this is Brod—," but I cut him off.

I grab his arm and clutch it. The words are poison. They come up with blood and guts and acid and, "I think Jena's dead."

19

If you want to see your father flip out:
an exercise in self-expression, honesty
and "psychological unlocking"
by Danielle Bailey

If you want to see your father flip out, then borrow his car and take it for a ride late at night, all without telling him. Oh, and spill blue smoothie on his leather passenger seat.

Things you might hear include: "What the hell, Fallen Child! This smoothie isn't even blueberry. It's blue for nothing."

Or "If I had known you were the one driving it, I'd have called the police sooner."

But if you want to see your father's face crumble and see him dizzy (but standing tall, strong, taking it like a man), if you want to prick every one of his molecules and make them bleed, then just tell him your fraternal twin is dead.

He might not have much to say for a minute, but when he gets it together, he gets it together. Let him lead you outside and calmly call your mother. She won't pick up her damn cell phone or the house phone, and you will curse her. Curse her curse her curse her because where the hell is she?

Your father drives drives drives down the slippery highway and doesn't say one word. Not one. Well, he says a few. He asks how you know and you tell him you just do. You felt it. Then hug yourself and let noisy tears fall, detouring to the tip of your nose before suicide-jumping off it.

Every time he starts to say something about how things will be okay and how he loves you and he's sure it's nothing, he stops. He doesn't know things will be okay. It doesn't matter that he loves you. It is not nothing.

You know this and have known this for many years, but today, right now, he's just figured it out. He knows nothing.

Maybe he thought he would save your sister, your mother, and you.

Today he knows he is, for lack of a better, more dad-friendly word, a fool. He cannot. And God willnot.

Five minutes away from your house, your mother calls. You hear her voice through the cell phone, falsely cheery, weak, and so guilty. She was just in the shower. Jena is asleep.

Everything is still the same.

Your father apologizes to you after he hangs up, even though you both know that it is really you who ought to apologize. You accept it anyway.

Somewhere deep inside he is very, very angry with you. Why did you pull the rug out from under him?

He tap tap taps all the way home.

Instead of coming in with you, he goes around the outside of the house and has his first cigarette in many, many months.

Feel proud.

This is how to see your father flip out.

There are other ways, of course, but this is the easiest.

On Monday after school, I refuse to answer a single one of Harry-with-an-*i*'s questions. For the first fifteen minutes, she prods and pokes, trying to wring words of any kind out of me. But when I'm confident she's ready to give up, she just starts rambling on about personal release and the freedom in *documenting* one's thoughts, and then she pushes a pen and notebook in front of me. Finally, when I hand this in at the end of the session, she has only one thing to say: "Why is psychological unlocking in quotation marks? Sure you don't need me to explain it to you again?"

"I just want my M&M's."

They are all peanut this time.

"What if I cut my hair?"

I am sitting on the carpet in Jena's room, running my fingers through my bangs. I should be doing homework and she should be napping, but since Saturday's freak-out, the hallway between our rooms feels like the English Channel. All the corners in this house are too far away.

"How short?" she asks.

"Short." I hold my fingers about an inch apart.

She is lying on her side facing me, and she cringes. "It takes a certain bone structure to pull that off. You don't have it."

I kick the foot of her bed. "Then I'll dye it, go lighter." *We'll look like twins.*

There's a family portrait in the dining room where we are wearing all white, a "natural" moment of familial bliss that was totally choreographed by Mom. Jena and I are seven and I am missing a front tooth, and she's been caught mid-blink, but it's the one picture that always makes people ask if we are identical.

"Please God, don't. The Baileys have endured enough hair catastrophes." *Namely hers*, she doesn't say, and we laugh.

"Keep your hair, Backup." And when she says that, I stop laughing, and I'm suddenly sure I don't want to keep my hair.

We are silent, except for her breath, always so loud. My soundless breath is a betrayal.

Then she says, quietly, "I need you to look like Dani. Please don't touch your hair."

And I know I won't.

20

I wake up thinking about the time I broke my arm, when I was ten.

It was Jena's idea for us to build a tree house because, even then, Mom's constant hovering was cramping her style. Although, of course, back then my mother hovered for different reasons. Or a different brand of the same reason, since she's always been afraid. I think that week she'd read about some kid who was stolen while his mother was waiting in line at the bank. In the weeks that followed, she barely let us out of her sight. Mom quizzed us on emergency phone numbers, pulled the plug on sleepovers, and checked on us multiple times during the night. It was good practice, I guess, but sometimes we just wanted to be left alone.

From all the way across the hall that summer morning, I could hear the muffled sounds of drawers opening and shutting, and Jena's window sliding up and down. *Up and down.* When I went into her room, Jena's first words to me were an order. "Shut the door." Her eyes followed my hands as they wrapped around the knob and the door snapped back into place. My sister had always been bossy, and if you didn't know much about us, you probably assumed Jena was older.

"What are you doing?" I asked.

"I'm building a tree house," she said matter-of-factly.

I stood there, staring at her. She'd spoken about a tree house before, but I hadn't expected her to *build one*. The last I knew of it, we were trying to convince Dad to help us make one. Maybe in the fall, when he had some time off work, he'd said.

Jena didn't like to wait. A small pile of resources was building up in front of her closet door now. Books, old crosswords and Archie comics, and the small radio that used to be Grandpa's.

"So where will the tree house be?"

"I'll show you," she said, and walked toward her window, slid it up, and then motioned for me to come on. It was the huge oak tree just outside her bedroom, the one Dad sometimes frowned up at and mentioned something about hiring people to trim or remove it altogether. He told Mom he didn't like the way one branch was leaning, and she mostly just acted uninterested and said there was a lot that needed taking care of, when he had time.

My sister had draped a bedsheet from a branch above the leaning one, so the cloth hung down like a curtain, forming the "walls" of the tree house. The leaning branch itself was the floor, where Jena planned to sit.

"I'm taking stuff up there now," she said, starting to fill an enormous tote bag with the radio and books that had been in front of her closet door. "Wanna come?"

At first, I just watched her. Her hair had been pulled back into a messy ponytail, and it went down just past her shoulders, frizzy and thick, the color of hazelnuts. Then, slowly, she went through the window, holding the frame around the glass for support, and cautiously stepped onto the tree's nearest branch. It was a sturdy branch, in no danger of breaking. And Jena had excellent balance. If Mom had been willing to take her to gymnastics—Jena wanted to do gymnastics, but Mom wanted her to compromise and take dance, so my sister decided on soccer—she might have had a promising competitive career.

By the time she'd come and gone twice both ways, I was starting to get into the idea of a tree house. Sure, it wasn't at all like the one I'd imagined Dad building for us, but it could be fun.

From our spot in the tree, we could hear Mom's mournful opera music travel throughout the house. We could hide up there with our crossword puzzles and leftover candy from our birthday, and watch the neighbors come and go without realizing that we saw every picked wedgie and nose, every cigarette smothered and mouth sprayed before going in to kiss a spouse. And Jena's tote bag, filled with the books and stuff from inside, hung down from the branch above us so we had basically everything we needed. This was going to be fun.

I didn't fall going up the first time. I was going back inside the house to get the half-pack of grape bubblegum on my nightstand. We could share it and compare bubbles as we enjoyed an afternoon of understated delinquency. But as I was walking along that branch, the branch that Dad complained leaned too close to the house, my ankle rolled a little to the right, and I fell.

I only twisted my ankle, but I broke my right arm, the one that *isn't* in a cast right now.

Jena cried as Mom drove us to the hospital. She told my mother in one rapid-breathed confession that it was all her fault and that she'd made me do it. I don't know if she thought she was protecting me, or why she felt she needed to.

I've never forgotten how much my arm hurt—not because it was any worse than anything I've broken since, but because it was the first time. And let's just say the discovery that humans are breakable was a monumental one for me.

I proudly displayed the X-ray on my wall for the next five years, the grays and whites and in-between colors shifting and twirling into one another. Mom took it down the week Jena was diagnosed. I suppose it would have been a little insensitive to leave it up, though I think the sight of my right arm, whole and normal and healthy while hers isn't, is a greater injustice.

I haven't thought about the time I broke my arm in years, not even after crashing Spencer's bike and breaking my wrist. But since I woke up, it's been all I can think about. And now, as I sit here in the library with Jack Penner, watching him work on our assignment, it *still* won't leave me.

And he notices. "You seem a little distracted."

"I know," I sigh. "I'm sorry. I'm usually so *present* and, like, involved."

Jack doesn't comment on that. "What are you thinking about?" As I turn to face him, he looks away, seemingly embarrassed to have asked the question. I'm not sure why. Why he asked, or why he's embarrassed.

"What are *you* thinking about?" I shuffle a little closer to him as he pulls the book on Great Mathematicians of the Past closer to himself.

"The assignment."

I pretend to consider this for a second. "In general, what do you think about?"

"In general?" he shrugs. "Everything. School. My family. My dog. My friends." He's still not looking at me.

I decide to give him a minute to return to his natural coloring, but he surprises me by breaking the silence. "You think about your sister a lot, don't you?"

"I can tell," he adds, quickly, "because that's when you're the most distracted."

I feel the back of my neck start to burn. I definitely liked Jack better when he was too afraid to talk to me. I *like* Jack better when he's too afraid to talk to me.

"I don't know, Jack," I whisper, moving even closer to him, letting my hand hang limply from the wrist, brushing his knee. There, that ought to make him shut up. "Right now, she's the furthest thing from my mind." I'm so close to him that I suspect the heat on my face is my breath bouncing onto his face and jumping back at me. So close that I don't remember his eyes ever being this gray or unflinching or cutting into mine as they are now. But I don't fully comprehend how close that is. Not until Jack's lips are brushing against mine and, behind the encyclopedias and the educational magazines nobody ever reads, he is kissing me. He's kissing me and his lips are soft and I can hear him breathing and me breathing and I think my left hand just fell off.

Fifteen seconds. That's how long I'd say it lasts, if I had to guesstimate. Then we're pulling apart and my hand won't stop shaking and Jack looks like someone painted him red. He stares at a spot in the carpet and begins to mumble something.

The words fall out of his mouth, still tainted by my breath. "I . . . didn't . . . I'm sorry . . ." Or at least, I think that's what he's saying.

But I interrupt him, so I can't be sure. "I've broken my arm before," I say, and why am I still shaking? "When I was ten. And I can't stop thinking about it."

Then I get up and leave him sitting there, embarrassed and stunned and anxious.

And even now, it's all I can think about. That time I broke my arm when I was ten. And not the fact that I just let Jack Penner kiss me. With his pant legs riding up, and his Star Wars socks exposed. And the possibility that I kissed him back.

21

But when I *do* allow myself to think about it, to *really think about it,* I want to kill myself. Which sounds better than it is.

He probably irons his jeans the night before school. And, God, his underwear. I bet he irons his underwear. Two days later, and this is all I can think about.

When the curiosity becomes too much, I tear a page from my empty math notebook and write: *Do you iron your jeans? And underwear?*

I fold it into quarters, then into more quarters, and I should know how many quarters that makes total (we are in math class, after all), but I don't. I slip my hand under the desk and hold it out to him. Then I watch him while he reads it. His face falls, because he was probably hoping it said something different. A romantic proposition about having his babies, or being his girlfriend at the very least.

Two minutes pass before he writes back, sliding the piece of paper across the small distance between our desks. His handwriting is neat and precise, like one would expect, even though his blue pen looks like it might be running out of ink.

My mom irons my jeans. Why?

No reason, I write back. At the front of the class, Halbrook stands with his back to us, writing in barely decipherable letters on the whiteboard.

I think we should talk and get it over with. I'm sorry about what happened, and I know you've been avoiding me.

I don't know why I ever thought it was a good idea to exchange notes with Jack during math class. Clearly, he has only one thing on his mind.

Disappointing. And here I thought he was different than all the other boys.

What do you mean we haven't talked? I thought I said hi at the start of class. Am I hallucinating again?

You did, but then you turned away before I could say anything back. Anyway, I didn't mean to kiss you.

I know—and after careful consideration, I've decided I won't be pressing charges.

I see him frown, two creases at the top of his forehead. He opens his mouth as if preparing to say something, then closes it again, remembering himself and where we are. It probably also occurs to him that there is no way I'm going to admit anything ever happened in a public forum. So, instead, he pulls out a black pen—his blue one has finally given up on life and, in turn, he has given up on it.

I think it's important to discuss things. It's always better, in my experience.

I glance up briefly to catch Lauren giving me a disapproving look. Ever since she came back from being suspended, she's been even more devout in her commitment to schoolwork. I make a point of pretending to copy down Halbrook's notes. I bet that's what everybody else is doing—pretending. The only two people in the world that ever truly understand anything that Halbrook does, not to mention writes, are Halbrook and Lauren. Jack might act like he does, too, but you can never really tell with him.

We ARE discussing things. Anyway, I'd think you'd be a little more relieved that I've decided to withhold legal action (for now). I'm not usually so forgiving when boys cram their tongues down my throat.

Jack's response is in front of me within seconds.

That's not really how it happened.

And then, before I've even had the chance to think about my reply, another piece of paper lands in front of me.

All right, fine. Let's not talk about it.

There's something inherently pissy about this note, even though it's barely two sentences long. It's in the way the letters on the page are more pointy than the ones before them, the way the *i*'s are dotted—intentional and angry and almost square.

When I glance over at him, Jack has his math face on again. His focus is completely on the board ahead, and his hands are dancing all over his page, replicating in small, neat letters the illegible squiggles Halbrook has on the board.

I squint, cock my head to the side, and struggle to see the way everybody else sees, the way Jack sees. But . . . nothing. Maybe I should get glasses.

You know when you walk into a room and you get the feeling that someone is talking about you *right now*? That's the sense I get, standing in the cafeteria at lunchtime. Or maybe it has something to do with the fact that volume control and general subtlety have never been Candy's strong suit. She is standing in the lunch line.

"I feel more sorry for her than anything," she is saying non-chalantly, shrugging as she brings a bottle of water to her lips. "If our roles were reversed, and by some imbalance in the universe *she* had Spencer, I would totally be breaking down in class, too, and, like, making out with geeks in the library."

Candy snort-laughs at her own joke, and the pack of girls surrounding her release their own set of hyena laughs.

My palms feel moist and sticky as I walk toward them.

"Oh," Candy says when she sees me coming. She diverts her gaze from mine and faces forward in line again. I go and stand right next to her, close enough that it's uncomfortable for both of us, but not close enough that I'm tempted to gag or hold my nose. I can't help it, I've always thought Candy smelled like mushrooms.

The girls that were cozying up to her just a second ago keep some distance between us and them, but don't leave entirely, afraid they'll miss some sort of throwdown. If it should come to that.

"Did you do something to your hair?" I ask her with a bright smile. "It looks washed."

She swallows, but doesn't answer.

"I really like it. I think the last time you had it like this was in ... third grade?"

Now she narrows her eyes at me. "I heard you and Jack were making out in the library." Her voice is unnaturally loud, even for Candy, and I feel her watching me closely, trying to measure my level of embarrassment.

"Well, I usually don't kiss and tell," I reply evenly, "but I'm happy to report that he doesn't have the same salivary condition Spencer has."

Candy folds her arms across her chest. "Like you've kissed Spencer. You're a liar."

"There's a fly stuck to your eyelashes."

"And a bitch," she hisses.

"And if you're going to wear a nose ring, you should really keep your nose in the air less. Things don't look quite right in there, you know?"

Her mouth falls open. Then, she seems to collect herself. "It's a *nasal septum piercing*, not a nose ring."

"Okay." I nod. "Again, not right. Did you know they sometimes just fall through? Spontaneously? And then they, like, break the—what did you call it—the septum?"

Everybody seems to be holding their breath. "Anyway," I smile, "you girls have a nice lunch. Say hi to Spencer for me, okay?"

Without waiting for her answer, I turn and walk away. Lauren is nowhere to be found and while I consider sitting with Jack for a nanosecond, he quickly shifts his gaze as soon as I catch it. When I'm walking past his table, I think I see him move his bag from the seat next to him, but I'm probably imagining things.

So I head to the library, pull out one book on various eye conditions and another on cats.

It's quiet in here, and deserted. Mrs. Uri, who hasn't seen me, sits huddled in her corner, reading one of those magazines she leaves out to inspire us, nibbling on a sandwich and breaking her own rule. Part of me wants to say something, since I'm in a confrontational mood today, but I end up just flipping idly through my books and watching her eat.

I feel like I truly understand her by the time the bell rings. And she's riveting. Especially the way she obsessively wipes down the surface of the table following each bite.

That's not all I'm doing, though. I'm also trying to figure out who saw and how and from where. It's funny how one can feel invisible and unseen, eating illegally in the library or letting one's lips be kissed by geeky boys, all the while totally unaware that you're being watched.

I bite into the flesh on the side of my mouth until it starts to bleed. I want to find a smaller space to hide, in between the shelves, or inside the pages of this book, or in between the letters of a word.

Five.

I want to fold myself inside out and disappear. Grow smaller, smaller, smaller, till nobody can see me.

22

The first boy to ever throw rocks at my window late at night is tall, with dark tufts of brown hair, eyes a little too close together, and a two-day shadow. He doesn't serenade me—he can't play the guitar—and he doesn't help me climb out, shushing me as I giggle, entangled by bushes and my own feet. This boy is hardly worth coming down for at all, but I owe him.

He's my father.

"Shh. I don't want to wake your mother." He breathes heavily, holding himself up on the ledge of the window by placing his full weight on his arms, like an upright, creepy-father version of push-ups.

I blink and try to undo the image. Where is Spencer and the boom box he will use to prove how sorry he is for picking Candy over me? Where is Johnny Depp? At this point, even Jack Penner would do. It's just my luck that it's my father, and he's refusing to disappear.

"I . . . got something. Will you . . . come down and see?"

There are so many things wrong with this scene, but all I say is, "I'll be right down."

He shushes me, but I'm already slamming my window shut, worming my way into clothes I can afford to be caught dead in—jeans, an oversized T-shirt, and my coat—and heading down the stairs.

Once out the front door, I head around the corner to the start of the driveway. Dad is leaning against the garage door staring straight ahead, his breathing still loud.

"I don't know if you've heard," I tell Dad, hugging my coat to myself, "but lack of sleep stunts growth. Particularly in adolescents."

"I'm sorry, hon. But I couldn't wait to show you this." My eyes follow Dad's to the end of our driveway, where a huge white RV sits, tires smothering a layer of decaying snow. "Well?"

I open my mouth and allow saliva to gather on the tip of my tongue, wetting my words so they slip out more easily and harden in the cool, wintery air.

"Dad," I say slowly.

"I know," he nods, as if I've already finished my impending lecture. "It's not a good time."

"And it's winter."

"And it's not at all sensible." He sounds like he's talking to himself, or maybe the RV, since he can't tear his eyes away from it. "But if not now, when? You know, why not right now? Everything feels like *now*."

He turns to look at me. "Do you like it?"

I don't say anything.

"There are beds and a kitchen and a TV. It's like being at home but smaller, cozier."

Is he trying to convince himself or me?

"My mother," I say slowly, my toes tingling where the cold air chews through my holey socks, "is going to kill you." Sure, Mom and Dad had been talking about renting an RV soon, but we all know that Soon is when we don't have to worry about starting off the trip with four and coming back with three. Soon is after—*if*—we get our miracle.

Dad laughs, runs a nervous hand through his hair. "I went to the RV store in the morning, fell in love, and let her spend the day at Rick's while I figured out what I'd say to your mother."

The obvious questions are which parts of the RV have Dad convinced it's a "her," and what exactly he figured he'd say to my mother. Instead, I say, "Rick?"

"Guy from work," he explains.

"So you waited until Mom was asleep to sneak out and bring it home?"

Dad looks sheepish but doesn't say anything.

We stand there for a long time, just staring out at the street, at the RV.

So. Dad wants to run away. Who would have thought?

He's still smiling. "It's cold. You go on inside so you don't catch something. And get some rest or you'll be falling asleep in class tomorrow."

"What about you?"

He shrugs. "Last day before I'm exiled. Might as well enjoy the outdoor sights—find the constellations, breathe in the wind."

"You're smoking again, aren't you?"

Dad sighs and looks down, sort of ashamed, but not quite. "Don't tell your mother."

I shuffle back inside, leaving Dad to plot his own method of escape. We all have ours. Mine apparently involve ill-advised makeout sessions. My mother's are God and my barely existent acting career. My father's are cigarettes and RVs. I don't know what Jena's are, but I'm sure she has some.

An hour or two passes, and I drift in and out of sleep. I hear the sound of the front door downstairs creaking open. Holding my breath, I listen to find out whether it's my father coming in or my mother, having woken up, going out to behead him.

When twenty minutes later I hear voices, I figure it's number two. Too bad I didn't ask how he feels about cremation while we were outside bonding.

Mom is speaking in a very controlled but firm voice.

I'm expecting a door to slam—the closest Dad ever comes to asserting himself—and I refuse to let myself sleep until I hear it.

Half an hour passes, though, and nothing. An hour.

My head hurts. Elephants march across my eyelids and they weigh down my eyelashes.

I dream that a boy comes to my window, throws stones,

and strums a sweet, homemade melody, inspired by me. His voice is husky, rich, and controlled; his kiss is anything but.

We giggle and breathe not-whole secrets, but whispers of secrets into the night. My hands melt into his strong, rough-but-not-farmer-rough hands.

The night envelops us in its warmth, a world where there is nothing but us and love and tonight and an eternity of more.

It's a good dream, but it's over too soon and then I'm remembering that no boyfriend of mine can do that now, because my father has tainted that particular fantasy.

I'm the last one to get up in the morning.

Why didn't anyone wake me?

I jump into the shower and get dressed for school. When I go downstairs, I accept Mom's offer to pour me a bowl of cereal. Jena sits across from me reading, and Dad is on his laptop. I search for rolled eyes behind backs, proof of the silent treatment, battle scars and traces of last night's "incident." Surely there were some.

"What are you staring at?" Jena asks, in turn staring at me.

"Do you know Dad rented an RV?" I ask loudly, still looking at my mom and dad, who are drinking a cup of coffee and typing away on a keyboard, respectively.

"Yeah, I do," she says.

I have plenty more questions: Did he throw snow pebbles at your window, too, and make you come out to see? Do you know if this means he now actually believes what he's been saying from the start, that you'll be okay, or does this mean he believes the marks all over your body, the way your limbs are loose and tired—like your bones are not only sick, but absent? Does he think things are getting better, or that they're about to get worse?

I don't ask any of those questions, but I find out answers that are actually useful.

Like, they had a slight "disagreement" when Mom woke up and found Dad outside caressing his RV (he was lucky he'd already put out his cigarette), but soon resolved the situation when they *stopped to listen to the other person's side.* Which means they probably had good makeup sex, something I do not need to think about this early in the morning. Or over my breakfast, for that matter.

The most important and shocking fact, though, is that Mom is not making Dad take it back.

We're going on vacation today. In an RV. In the middle of winter.

23

It's the perfect way to spend time together," Dad keeps saying after breakfast, as if he's on repeat, a hopeful grin plastered on his face.

The rest of us follow in submission, dutifully preparing for the next three days, and silently thinking of ways to avoid one another. In truth, I should be ecstatic, since I'm missing school today for this, but somehow I can't conjure up any enthusiasm.

Dad does most of Mom's packing, while she makes a million phone calls and last-minute trips to the pharmacy.

"The key word," Dad says, "is minimalism. Don't take anything you won't need this weekend."

Jena wanted to pack her own stuff. I'm not sure what's happened to her, but today she actually told Mom to *back off and let her be.* Those were her exact words. Mom was stunned, of course. Disoriented. What was she supposed to do now? Eventually, she fluttered off to make sure we'd bring Jena back in one piece (see: the never-ending pharmacy runs), which, really, one can only be grateful for. Dead-person stench within the confines of an RV would not bode well.

Dropping my second bag on the ground, I head to the living room.

Mom is sitting with the phone in her lap, staring straight ahead. If I keep my head down and walk briskly, maybe she won't—

"Oh, hey." She glances up at me, a small smile on her face. "You all ready?" The corners of her lips spasm and I realize that she is working hard to keep her smile in place.

"Why are you letting us go?" I ask, before I think better of it.

"What do you mean?" She frowns, still somehow managing to keep the smile intact. "It's been a rough couple of months. We could all do with a break."

"But what about Jena?"

"What about Jena?" Speak of the girl and she will appear. Her one duffel bag hangs from her shoulder. She drops it to the ground beside mine and my eyes remain there. I wonder if she packed so light so she could carry her own bags.

Mom is up now, moving toward her. "Feeling better?"

"I was fine before." She turns to me now, speaking pointedly. "I'm sick, not dead."

"Don't be silly," Mom scolds. "Nobody said that. Do you want a glass of milk with your pills?"

My sister rolls her eyes. I leave her and Mom in the living room, their voices bristling, clashing, but still too timid to throw any real punches.

In my room, I find a bunch more stuff I want to take with me. I pack a third bag and bring it downstairs.

"Danielle," is Dad's expression of disapproval. "Did you see how little your sister packed?"

"Exactly," I say. "I want to *minimize* our waste of space. Besides, you never know when you'll feel like listening to some Van Faling. And I can't fall asleep without Mr. Blankie."

"What are you, five?" Jena asks.

Ignoring her, I continue, "I also packed a few boxes of tampons because lately, I've been a bit irregular."

Dad coughs. "You can take the bag. Jena, sure you don't want to add anything else? This is your last chance."

"Eric." Mom reappears from the dining room, clutching the Jena Book. It's a hardback black notebook that travels between my mother and sister, documenting each medical issue or near-issue, and any mother-daughter secrets they've got between the two of them. "Was it last Thursday or Friday we had the meeting with Dr. Leon?"

"Friday," Dad answers. Then, "My God, Dani, what did you put in this bag?" before he heads down the hall and out again.

As morning turns to afternoon, Mom suddenly realizes that Jena won't live without food either, so she tries to convince Dad that we should wait till tomorrow morning and leave bright and early. "There's no way we can get everything together in just one day. It's unreasonable."

Dad says nothing, his face flushed from all the heavy lifting (mine) he's spent the last hour doing and the cold.

Now, I think. *Here it comes.*

I'm pretending to watch TV, some lame game show where the host has an unfortunate receding hairline and a faux Australian accent, but am inwardly thinking: *Fight! Fight! Fight!*

My responsible father, who has spent the last sixteen years chastising my mother's crazy whims and spur-of-the-moment decisions, has spent all of five minutes putting together the family trip we've been planning for years. My eccentric mother is being rational and not jumping at the thought of spending an entire three days with her workaholic husband and lost-cause children.

Maybe I'm wrong, but I'm assuming they want their predetermined roles back.

Instead, though, Dad's expression softens. "What if I help? We could all pitch in."

My mother sighs, blowing up her bangs. "We'll see."

I'm forced to get up and help, too. When we finish in about ten minutes, I wonder if that wasn't Mom's last "attempt" at stopping this trip. It still doesn't make much sense to me. Jena's barely been allowed outside since she got sick, and now it's fine for her to go camping? Granted, both my parents will be there to keep an eye on her. But still.

"God, you need to stop staring," Jena says. "It's widely regarded as rude."

"So did you get bad news or something?"

"You mean because of the trip?" she asks.

I nod.

"Nothing has changed. Is that good or bad?"

"Subjective," I mumble with a shrug. Then I sneak into Mom and Dad's bathroom upstairs and open the cabinet where Mom keeps the sleeping pills she doesn't use. I smuggle them downstairs, add them to my bag of toiletries. Just in case something goes wrong while we're gone; in case Jena needs me.

"All right, Bailey women!" Dad cries out. "Ready to head off on the Great Adventure?"

His gusto, and Mom's poor attempt at it, more than make up for my and Jena's lack of enthusiasm. Although, by the time we get into the RV and Dad has given us the "deluxe tour" of what is to be our home for the next three nights, my sister starts to brighten.

She loves being outdoors, getting dirty, hiking, roughing it.

How did I forget that?

"Don't tell Dad," she whispers confidentially, sitting on the bed we're supposed to share, "but this might not totally suck."

How did I forget that, and she's not even dead yet?

24

It's late afternoon when we set off, and by the time we arrive, it is dark outside. The RV park we're staying at is only four hours away from home—*in case of emergency*, they don't say—but somehow Dad and Jena have managed to convince themselves that this is the equivalent of backpacking through South America.

Mom tries, too, but there's a reason she retired from acting.

After dinner, Dad roasts marshmallows with his lighter, which just *happened* to be on him when we needed it. (He mumbles about not having dry-cleaned his jacket in years, which I think Mom buys. She's tuned herself into believing the impossible, after all.)

Mom makes popcorn and, since it's too late to do anything else tonight, we squeeze onto the sofa at the back, buttered popcorn slipping between our fingers and landing under our feet. We watch old sitcom reruns and laugh at appropriate times.

I laugh, too, waiting for Jena to fall asleep next to Mom. Dad will have to carry her into the bedroom and tuck her into our oven-bed, where it's too hot for me under six blankets but too cold for Jena under five blankets, and she'll melt into a puddle because my warmth won't be able to reach her.

She doesn't fall asleep, though.

Mom does.

She sleeps for almost an hour, after which she wakes and starts apologizing profusely, like it's some kind of failure on her part, leaving Jena unattended. Dad tells her not to be silly and sends her to bed. I don't know if she sleeps again, but the three of us drink hot chocolate and play cards, whispering so we don't wake her.

Then Dad goes back to the sofa and watches late-night news. I stick my iPod earphones in and Jena goes to the front of the RV, reappearing a couple of minutes later with her book. I try not to make it obvious that I'm watching her. She scribbles for a long time.

Scribble scribble, scratch scratch.

I turn up my music so I can't hear.

Scribble scribble. Scratch scratch.

She still hasn't stopped writing.

Scribble. She chews on the pencil, squints. *Scribble scribble.*

She must hurt in a lot of places.

I wonder which are the ones I can see.

Dad goes out sometime in the morning to "explore" the park.

"What day is it?" Jena asks.

"Saturday," Mom replies, even though I'm one hundred

percent sure Jena was addressing me and not her. It's disturbing to think that my mom can hear what we're saying in our "bedroom" from the front.

Mom is walking back toward us now, holding a steaming cup of coffee, her hair pulled back, ready for the day.

"How are you girlies feeling?" she asks.

"Homesick," is my answer.

Mom smiles. "Well, that's a legitimate ailment. What about you, Miss Jena?"

"Really good."

"Really?" Mom straightens, her voice hopeful and worried all at the same time. "Better than yesterday?"

Jena nods. "I feel good. Maybe it's all the fresh air."

They laugh at this—Mom the loudest—because, of course, we've barely gotten any fresh air. If anything, we've been even more cooped up and isolated than usual.

Jena gets out of bed, takes a shower, and proceeds to plant herself in front of the TV, relieving me of five blankets. The sound of clanking and cheerful conversation makes it clear that Mom is in a good mood. A good Jena day is a good Mom day. A good Mom day is a good Dad day.

I pull the blanket over my head and try to tune them all out. Why do people always feel like nothing can go wrong just because they're having a good day? It's like the assumption that if you accomplish a goal you've set, the fat in your Kit Kat reward bar won't go straight to your hips.

"Guess what?" Dad's voice travels all the way from the

front. "The people who own the campground have invited us to come over."

Mom, Dad, and Jena talk among themselves. It seems Dad wants us all to go out and socialize. Mom, predictably, is less keen. "It's too cold to be gallivanting outdoors."

I manage to tune out their conversation. What I can't tune out, though, is Dad's voice, which appears to hover right over me.

"Wake up, sleepyhead, or the whole day will pass without you."

I haven't heard a better proposition in a long time so I stay put, unmoving. He shakes me awake. "Dani?"

"Some of us," I hiss, "are trying to sleep."

"You can take a nap after we get back."

Accepting that I can't compete with his enthusiasm, I groan. "Fine. I'll come and meet you guys after I shower."

"Great," Dad says, clapping his hands. "Jena, you ready?"

Mom and Dad discuss her coat and its warmth, or lack thereof. Then the door of the RV closes and they're gone.

After a quick and barely-warm shower, I'm heading to the kitchen to find something to eat when the door bursts open and Dad walks in.

"There you are! I started to think you weren't coming." He grabs the camera off the sofa. "Wanna hear something crazy?"

"We've gone back in time and are now in something B.C."

Dad laughs. "Nope. Even your mom would agree that it's not quite cold enough to be Canada."

I stare at him.

He rolls his eyes. "I was joking. Misinformed parents do that sometimes . . . What, you thought your sense of humor was some freak mutation?"

"Dad," I say, "this is the official end of this conversation. What is your something crazy?"

"Two things, actually," he says as I grab a muffin and start to follow him out of the RV. "One, the owners are taking us ice-fishing! Two, there's this kid here that knows Jena."

"No shit," I mumble.

"Danielle, really."

"Mmhmmhmm."

Dad assumes it's an apology. "Yeah. They're a great family. The boy's the same age as you two. He goes to your school."

It's right then that I start to get this strange feeling. Not the kind you get when there's nonstop rain and there is no God, or when you're walking into a dungeon of lions and there is no God.

"His name is Jake, I think. Or Jack. Something like that."

It's more the realization that there is a God.

And He's out to get me.

25

Outside our RV, there is a rug of dirty yellow snow sweeping over the ground like ten-year-old powder on a great-aunt's face. Snatches of highway appear between a patch of trees, and the only other objects in sight are two buildings several hundred feet from our RV.

"Apparently this is where they host big groups and retreats," Dad is saying as we reach the door of the bigger building. I'm assaulted by a wave of warmth as I go in after him. It looks like a cafeteria inside, spacious and dimly lit, with those blue fluorescent lights people convince themselves work. Two round tables are pushed close together with chairs around them.

Mom and Jena are sitting with a group of people. My eyes scan their table, then the one shoved next to it, for Jack. But I don't see him.

"Well, hello! You brought another one." From close-up, I realize that the man who is talking is not actually sitting on a plastic white chair like everyone else, but in a wheelchair.

Dad laughs. "Gareth, this is our other daughter, Danielle."

I smile and shake his outstretched hand. "Nice to meet you." The man has a round face, with silver sideburns and strong hands, like maybe he was a builder or professional athlete when he was younger.

There are five other people at tables—two women, another man, and a boy and girl around age nine and seven, respectively.

I run my right hand over my cast, feeling strangely self-conscious.

Once the introductions are over, I come back to stand behind Mom's chair. Dad is chatting to the other man and Jena is, as usual, beside Mom. I notice she's wearing two winter coats—hers and Mom's.

"Oh, good man!" Gareth says. "He's got more chairs. Danielle, I believe you know my son, Jack."

I turn around and he's standing there, a pile of chairs in front of him. His usually neat, academic hair looks like it's fought and lost a battle with the wind, and his eyes don't quite meet mine as he lifts a chair from the pile.

"Hi," I say, holding my hand out to him. "I'm the Other Daughter."

Everybody laughs, except Jena, because she doesn't like the way I phrased that sentence (even though I'm only repeating what Dad said), and me, because it's unfortunate to laugh at your own jokes, and Jack, because I think he understands that I'm calling a truce. We're not at school. We're in the awkward meet-the-family stage, where both of us have our relations to embarrass us, without me adding to it.

His hand wraps around mine, moving it in a surprisingly firm shake.

The laughter subsides as new conversations crop up and our hands untangle.

"Thanks for the chair," I say as he pulls another one from the stack and sets it on the ground. It's weird that he's sitting by me almost voluntarily. It's weird that Jena keeps looking over her shoulder, staring at us. It's weird that Jack's mom and my mom are talking, but not about me and how I've made her son's life miserable for the past sixish years and, by the way, why has Jack done all the work for that math assignment he and your daughter have?

Talking is the perfect filler, for silence, averting questions, awkwardness. Now, if I could only think of something appropriate to say. So far, I have:

So, sexy beast, you couldn't live a couple days without me, could you?

And:

Have I ever told you that you look adorable when your natural glow isn't obstructed by the glare of the whiteboard?

And:

Personally, I think it's still early on to meet the parents, but what do you think? Could you see yourself at Thanksgiving dinners' forever-and-ever amens?

"So, what are you doing here?"

I'm pissed Jack beat me to it, especially since given enough time and with some luck, I might have come up with it myself.

"We're winter RVing," I say. "Apparently, it's the latest holiday fad."

"I thought those were staycations . . . or something." He stares down at his lap.

A feeling that is equal parts surprise and pride hits me. "Jack."

"Yeah?"

"Did you just make a joke?" His lips tilt up, sheepishly. "I mean, practice makes perfect, but *bravo!*"

This time he laughs, a rich, deep sound that dances around us in the air, gentle, unobtrusive.

"Thanks. Well, I guess this explains why you weren't at school Friday. I mean, I wondered where you were." Pause. "My aunt and uncle own this place. They live round the back," he says, pointing to *round the back*, which I assume is the second building Dad and I saw, coming in. "We used to come here all the time in the summers and even in winter. My dad's a huge fan of ice-fishing."

I note the similarity, for the first time, between Jack's dad and the younger man, who must be his brother, sitting two seats from him.

"Are you?"

Jack shakes his head. "Not really. The most fun I have on these trips is trying to start a fire."

I open my mouth to speak. "Without matches," he says, before I can. His voice drops a little. "I guess Dad was in a nostalgic mood, so we decided to come out here for the weekend."

My eyes wander across the table, where Gareth is talking animatedly, his laugh loud and strong. I wonder if he had an accident or something.

"Listen," I begin, "I really have to apologize about our project. Only now that I see you do I remember that you wanted me to find pictures. I have this weird condition."

"Selective memory?" Jena chips in. We're sitting about five feet away from her, but I didn't realize she was listening to our conversation. Thank God I didn't say anything compromising. Or of an about-that-kiss nature.

Jack shakes his head. "Don't worry about it. And let's not talk about school."

Or the Kiss. Or the fact that the last time I saw you, you wrote me a note with a subliminally pissed-off message.

"Who's talking about school?" Gareth has wheeled over so he's next to Jack now. "We're going ice-fishing! Who's talking about school?"

"Nobody," Jack says.

"*Who's* talking about school?"

Jack grins. "Nobody," he and Jena say at the same time, while I watch, mildly amused.

"There's a lake close by," Jack explains, delving into the history of the thing and how wide and deep it is, etc., but I'm only pretending to listen. I always imagined, being the über-geek he is, that he'd have come from some really uptight, academic lineage, where his family ate together every night while watching CNN (I mean, if they owned a TV), and his parents still maintain that he's too young for the birds-and-the-bees talk. Meeting the Penners, however, suggests an entirely different situation and a more troubling one, at that. It appears that Jack owes one hundred percent of his chronic geekiness to himself and no one else.

We all stand, feeding off Dad's and Gareth's enthusiasm, making plans to meet in an hour for the Great Ice-Fishing Escapade, after everyone's dressed for the cold. Even Jena and Mom plan to go.

"Hey, Dani," Jack says as I push my chair back and start to follow Dad. "You're planning to come, right?"

Before I can answer, Jena jumps in yet again. "Of course she is."

"Good." And he actually seems to mean it. "I can show you how to light a fire. I mean, without matches. In case you ever need it."

Jena stares at him, amused. Mom's arm slithers around her, wrapping her in reality and dragging her away from me.

I follow.

26

Jena has decided that Jack is in love with me. I think she's trying to get me back for attempting to set her up with Rufus.

She sits on the bed, her top coat unzipped. "Did you see how happy he was when you said you were coming fishing?"

"'Happy' is a strong word. I'd call it more 'resigned.'"

Her expression falls slightly as she senses that my walls are up and she's not nearly strong enough to climb over. Not even today when she is leukemia's version of Superwoman.

She's not ready to concede, though. She has other plans.

Today, we will act like regular sisters, gossiping about boys and crushes and sharing feelings. We will make up for months upon months of not talking about anything so we didn't have to talk about It. We will make up for years upon years, the ones we might miss. Now is all we have. Let's be sisters today.

"Jena? I need to take your temperature!" Mom calls from the front.

Jena pulls herself up, her bones creaking and howling and giving her away, even when her heart is strong and her will is kick-ass and her temperature is "Perfect! What did I say about God looking out for you, missie?"

Dad is not in the RV. When he returns a few minutes later, slightly on edge, and brushes his teeth while Mom is busy praising God and hugging Jena, I figure he's a bonafide smoker once more, a backsliding, deceptive husband. Yet another statistic to add to our many.

I intentionally brush his shoulder as he advances from the bathroom smelling entirely too minty not to be suspicious. I mean, if Mom was concerned with anyone but Jena.

Insisting she doesn't want to take any chances, Mom packs a bag full of medical supplies—in addition to your basic first-aid kit—and nearly forgets Jena. I remember, though, and walk behind her the whole way there.

The day passes in a bit of a blur. Unsuccessful attempts at ice-fishing (Dad). Questions about the legality of our activities (Jena). Then, of course, the starting of fires.

Technically, Jack starts all but three. Two sort of belong to Jena. I'm not particularly enthusiastic about the whole thing, especially since it's too cold for them to last more than a couple of seconds anyway.

"Sure you don't want to try?" Jack offers for about the sixteenth time this hour. Jack is different than I imagined. He's confident when he knows what he's doing. He also never gets too far away from his dad, helping him maneuver unleveled paths and hauling around stuff so Gareth doesn't have to put anything on his lap.

"I'm positive."

"Oh, come on," Jena says, still looking smug over the fact that she successfully accomplished this one thing—the second fire on only her third attempt. "Once upon a time there was a chicken called Danielle."

I glare at her. "She attacked a fool named Jenavieve."

"There's no need to name call." My sister shrugs her weak shoulders, playing with a circle of snow she picked up from the ground beside her. "Whatever. Can I have another turn, Jack?"

Jena and Jack seem to have hit it off. Not in a romantic way, I don't think, but in that way you act when friends or cousins come over and you haven't had guests in a long time and don't want them to ever leave. That's Jena. Jack? Well, I suppose he's happy just to be wanted. And, according to my sister, to be around me.

At some point, I'm not sure when, I give in and agree to light a fire. Except I'm really particular about it not burning out. So as soon as a tiny blue flame appears, and Jena and Jack ooh and ahh over the little creature, I bend over it, fencing it in with my hands and urging it to last just a little longer. I even— and I'm not proud of this—feed it the sleeve of Dad's coat, the one he let me wear because he got too hot and I try to help out where I can. For a second, it appears to work, but then Jena is yelling.

"Oh my God, Dani, what are you doing? You can't do that."

Jack is equally stunned. "That's really dangerous . . . and isn't that your dad's?"

I stub the sleeve into the ground to put out the fire. Then I go back to hovering over my flame, willing it to live and to resist the cold, the force of the wind, the pull back into the earth where it melts and it's like it never existed.

But slowly, surely, it dissolves, eating at itself, growing smaller and smaller. I can't fan it back to life. Do I leave it and let it die? Or fight fight fight to make it burn?

In the end, it doesn't matter.

I can't do anything. Nothing to save it.

Jack and Jena are no longer saying anything, just watching me.

I try to pull my throat out of my stomach. "Well," I say, but my voice comes out like more of a whisper. "That sucked."

"Yours lasted the longest," Jack offers.

"I try," I say, flopping down to the cold ground, holding the burned sleeve of Dad's coat out to Jena. "Can I say you did this? I mean, I doubt he'll disown you, in your condition."

"I think," Jack says, "that we should attempt some ice-fishing. I'm not very good, but I'll show you guys."

"Sounds like a plan, Jack."

"Yeah," I agree. "Let's ice-fish."

And we do, except we don't catch anything. Jena starts to cough and the tip of her nose, plus the bit between her nostrils and her upper lip, reddens. I'm glad Mom's pills are at the bottom of Bag Three. I watch Jena closely, trying to determine if she'll need me, need my life today. Mom wants us to hurry up and get inside please. Dad makes his apologies and we round up to leave.

"Dani?" Jack stops me as I turn to go. "I'm glad . . . I mean, I had a good time today. You're . . . your family is nice."

"I'll tell them." I smile, feeling relieved for him that it's just me he's talking to, and not a real girl. I mean, a girl he has a chance with.

"Well," I say, hoping Jack understands that I'm saying goodbye.

"Um, about Thursday," he begins, *clearly* not understanding. He shifts the cooler he's holding from his left hand to the right. "I'm sorry, I didn't mean to be rude in the note," he says. I fight the urge to tell him that he wasn't, I'm just observant. "It just bothers me when people pretend like everything is okay when it's not."

His tone suggests that statement is not exclusively directed at me. "If that's supposed to have some deep and profound meaning, I don't get it."

He seems to consider whether or not to say more. "My dad," he says finally, staring at the handle on the cooler. "It's been more than a year since the accident, and I don't think he's talked about it once."

My eyes travel to Gareth, who is several feet away from us, laughing about something with his brother. "Maybe it was traumatizing."

"Well, he acts like it was no big deal, like it never even

happened. He doesn't like me to know when he's in pain. I guess he thinks it makes him weaker or something."

All I can think is that Jack shouldn't be telling me this. We don't even really know each other.

"And then," he continues, "he gets all ambitious and wants to go ice-fishing. In the fall, he wanted to take his wheelchair on one of the easier trails we used to hike. We didn't even make it halfway."

His voice is soft and sad and pricks my fingers and throat.

"He tries to hide it but it makes him really frustrated and depressed." Jack sighs. "Sometimes I think it would be easier if we were all more honest about what we can and can't do. It's not a sign of failure if you can't do something."

I'm staring at Gareth again and thinking about his strong hands, the square, muscular shape of shoulders that act as arms and feet. What can't he do? "What can't *you* do?"

Jack considers the question for a second. "Um, well," he says, "no matter how precise I try to be, visualizing the trajectory and path of a basketball, I can never seem to get it into the hoop. At least not without a couple of misses first."

I decide not to inform him that I have no idea what *tra-jeck-to-ree* means. "That's terrible, Jack. How can you even look at yourself in the mirror?"

He grins. "And most people think I'd be good at video games, but I'm not. I'm awful, actually." A short laugh escapes him. "And sometimes I write down stuff to say to you in the margins of my Spanish notebook, and I can never remember it."

My head snaps up. "Wait, what? What kind of stuff?"

"Um . . ." His face flushes. "I don't know. Stupid stuff. Like, 'How was your weekend' or 'I like your new haircut' or 'I . . .'" He appears to change his mind about the last sentence and his voice fades. "Just stuff like that."

My teeth are gnawing on the inside of my cheek and Jack's face looks like it's burning, and probably we're both in pain. I shouldn't have asked, but I was curious, and now I'm supposed to say something.

"Hey, can I ask you something?" I say, which a) is a total placeholder and completely defeats the purpose, and b) I don't wait for his reply, which also defeats the purpose. "Have you ever thought about Jena?"

"Like . . . what?" He looks confused. "How do you mean?"

I temporarily stop nibbling on my cheek so I can answer. "She's really pretty." And almost as soon as I've stopped, I want to go back to it, to digging my teeth into the inside of my face. "Especially when she's not wearing sixteen jackets."

Jack doesn't say anything; he stares down at his hands. Maybe he's trying to make his mouth bleed, too.

For some inexplicable reason, I get this urge to rewind and take it back, or say something nice, or maybe, maybe, even see if his lips remember mine. But my feet are already leading me away from him, and I don't know what I'm bad at, but I know what I'm good at: stomping all over the hearts of nerdy boys. *And I can be honest about it, Jack.*

"See you on Monday," I call over my shoulder, then hurry

away before he has more to feel embarrassed about. I don't know why I care. I guess because Jack Penner is actually sort of a nice guy. And nice guys deserve nice girls. And nice girls get cancer, and lose their chance at happiness.

The wannabe nice girl steps aside and waits for them to get better so they can live happily ever after with boys that are good for them.

She hurries to catch up with her family.

Thankfully, Jena does not ask about Jack again. She goes to bed early. She says she's not unwell, just tired, so maybe I won't need the pills tonight.

I slip into bed at eleven, after watching a late-night talk show with Dad, while Mom reads some booklet she apparently got at Jena's last appointment.

The last thing I expect to hear is Jena's voice, a soft whisper against the blanket of darkness. "Do people ever talk about me at school?"

I hear her breathing slowly, waiting for the answer. *In, out, in, out.*

"I didn't know you were awake."

In out in out. In.

She's waiting.

"Sometimes."

"They ask you?"

In. Out. In. Out.

"Yeah."

It's because of Jack. That's why she's asking all these questions, suddenly thinking about life outside of It, the life she had before and the one she'll have if there's an after.

"Do you remember Teddy's funeral?" She doesn't wait for me to answer, but I do remember. Teddy was this guy Jena befriended during chemo treatments. She begged me to go with her and Mom to his funeral in December. To support her and hold her hand, keep my shoulder squared so when she needed to sob into it, we wouldn't collapse onto each other or the people on either side of us. It was the first funeral either of us had been to. There was no ghost sighting, no open casket or dead-person smell. It wasn't a big deal.

"Everyone there was either related to him, treating him, or sick, too," Jena says.

If I'm supposed to say anything now, I fail.

"That's probably how my funeral will look."

I fail with distinction.

"Mom would kill me if she heard me say that."

"So why would you?" I hear myself asking, before I decide to.

"Because it's true. I didn't say I *would* die. I said my funeral would look like Teddy's if I did."

"Well, then don't." My voice muffles into my pillow and away from her, but I'm sure she hears it, too.

She doesn't answer right away, silence settling in between us, loud and haunting. Maybe it's too late. Maybe she has died already.

"If I die, you can have all my stuff."

My lips are glued together.

"You know you're the only person I'd ever trust with my things. My trophies, my clothes, my room. I know you hate when I talk like this but just in case . . . I think you should know."

Pause.

"It's weird, but I don't mind talking about it. It's not that I'm not scared—I am—but I guess I'm kind of used to it now. When I have a fever or I throw up or have a bad day, Mom automatically thinks that's it, that this is the end and I'm going to die right now. You can tell by her face."

The word-vomit keeps coming, like something in her has come undone and now she just wants to tell me anything and everything and she can't stop.

"The weird thing is that, to me, I never feel like it's the end. I mean, obviously, that's a good thing and I *shouldn't* feel that way. Maybe it's because I've thought I was dead or nearly dead so many times—when everything hurts and I'm sure I have to die now, because how can there be something worse? But I'm still here. So I don't know what it feels like to die."

Silence. Beautiful silence.

My lips stay together.

Hers don't. They quiver as words continue to fall from them, dribble that slides out and wets her pillow and mine and why can't she please just stop?

"I'm scared for you, Dani," she whispers. "And Mom and Dad. I think you guys worry too much and you take everything too seriously and you've given up too much." She sniffs. "I hate myself for being sick. Almost as much as you hate me."

My lips part so I can breathe.

In. Out. In. Out.

"I don't hate you."

"Yeah, right. You hate being around me." She double sniffs, a wheeze from her chest up. "I'm gross and ugly and weak and I'm ruining your life."

You're not ruining my life. I am.

You're not gross or ugly or weak. You are stronger than I am.

And:

I love you.

And:

Promise me you'll wake up every day I wake up.

"Lives," I say instead. "My *lives*."

Wrong answer, Dani. Wrong. Wrong. Wrong.

You are weak. *You* are gross.

I know she's not sleeping because I hear her softly breathing and trying to bat away the tears. As soon as the spaces between her breaths are regular, I climb out of bed and head to the bathroom.

There my lips part and they explode and they can't stop.

I'll die if you die.

That I did say. I said it when she had the chicken pox at age six, and I'd never had it, so we hadn't been allowed to see each other for three days. A bright kid even then, I snuck out of

Mom-sanctioned quarantine and up the stairs into her room, where since Jena's unfortunate diagnosis Mom had ensured I didn't set foot. She was itchy and cranky and I slid into her bed, offering to scratch her arm or read to her or make up a good Once Upon a Time. I was promptly discovered by Mom and had a red, splotchy chest area two days later, *after* Jena was beginning to feel better.

I said it again nine years later, sitting outside on the swings by our house, while Mom and our aunt Tish talked in quiet, serious voices and took great care to dab at their eyes only when a particularly strong wind blew.

She doesn't know how much I meant it then. I tiptoe into our room and find the bag. Back in the bathroom, I dig around for the bottle. When I find it, I uncap it and begin to count.

One. Two. Three . . .

What do I need five lives for?

She doesn't know how much I mean it now.

four

27

The good news is, nobody finds me facedown, heart-dead, drowning in a puddle of vomit, after I black out. The bad news is, I find me that way.

The bad news is, my stomach won't stop trying to jump out of my throat and expelling its contents.

The bad news is, Mom doesn't sleep and wanders to the bathroom when she hears all the flushing and hacking and so forth.

"Jena?" She knocks on the door. "Jena? Why the hell did you lock this? Open up! Let me in!"

She's just about to bang down the door, when the real Jena stands up. "I'm in bed. What's going on?"

"Oh my God. I thought I heard you in there throwing up. Are you okay? Are you sure?"

"I'm fine. Where's Dani?"

There's momentary silence as they both try to locate my whereabouts. Since I can't hear him moving, I assume Dad isn't about to break his record as the only one in our family who still sleeps.

"Dani?" Jena knocks on the door.

I'm still testing out my voice, so it takes me a moment to call back, "Yeah?"

"You okay, honey?" Mom asks.

"It must just be something I ate."

The bad news is, it starts again.

"Want me to come in?" Mom asks.

"No. It's . . . nasty."

Mom sends Jena back to bed, then waits outside my door as I attempt to get myself together. Five minutes and no throwing up. I take this as a good sign, stash the rest of Mom's pills in the cabinet so she will think Dad brought them and Dad will assume she did.

"You okay?" Mom presses the back of her hand to my forehead as soon as I open the door. "You don't look so good."

"I'm okay," I answer. While Mom prepares me a salt-and-water mixture (supposedly to keep the food down), I can't help thinking about the irony that is my life. The most fitting occupation for my mother is no longer a stage actress or momager or anything like that; she would make—she is—a fantastic nurse.

She checks on Jena once more, then has me come and sit on the couch with her as she channel surfs. Finally, she turns off the TV and we sit there in the silence, my body pressed against hers, stealing her warmth. As I lie there focusing on breathing and getting my stomach to stop swirling, it becomes overwhelmingly clear to me that she is stronger than I thought.

It's not just a front; a front could not hold me up tonight, while I shiver inside as everything within me threatens to spill out onto the floor.

She buries her chin in my hair and I fall asleep, feeling less myself and more like Jena.

Five lives down, four to go.

In the morning, Dad finds me in Mom's arms, huddled against her like she's the highest part of a ship that's going down.

He shakes her first and then me, telling us both to get up, get up, we need to see this.

What's wrong? we both think, but only Mom says it, brushing me off her lap.

"Where's Jena?" Mom asks.

"Outside," he answers.

"She's not sick, is she?" *Want me to answer that?* "Dani had food poisoning last night. It's strange we didn't all get it."

"Ah, I wondered about the setup," Dad says as Mom pulls on her coat and makes her way out of the RV. "Feeling better, kiddo?" His hand ruffles my hair, then settles on my shoulder.

"Yeah. What's outside?"

Dad grins. "You'll see." So I know it's good. Or he thinks it's good.

When I reach the last step of the RV, I freeze. Someone used a cotton wool machine to spray the world with fake snow.

It silently falls from the gray sky above, dancing: twirly, cold balls of cotton that land strategically on the ground, filling all the spaces where patches of ground and dead yellow snow once lay. I wonder who else is seeing this.

"Isn't it beautiful?" Jena calls from where she is, kneeling beside the RV and picking up handfuls of the stuff with her bare red hands. Mom notices and pulls out gloves from her coat pocket, handing them to my sister.

"Magical. This is the perfect way to end our vacation," Dad answers.

Mom nods, looking up at the sky. "God knew we needed a little snow."

There's something so childlike, so naïve about the way my mother says it. It's a sweet sentiment, that God saw us with our rotting snow, the fungus of our winter, and wanted to give us something new, beautiful, soft, and white. But there's something so wrong about it, too. My sister is dying; snow is the last thing we need right now.

It seems suspiciously like a cop-out on His part that that's what we get. And I can't believe they're all falling for it.

"Maybe," Dad says, "we should stay for one more night. I mean, it might even be dangerous to try to go back tonight."

"It's hardly a snowstorm, honey," Mom replies.

"I know." His smile is sheepish, see-through. "But I don't want to leave just yet." He steals a glance at Jena, who is quietly still scooping up bits of snow and letting them soak into the woolen gloves Mom handed her. This moment is a little like stepping into a time warp, an alternate universe where we have the memories of scars and battles and bleeding bones, but somehow we've managed to leave them behind. In this world, we get a bite-size, if not full, serving of hope.

The Baileys are greedy and they want more.

Always want more. More time. More Jena. More smiles. More happiness.

Greedy, greedy pigs.

Dad has his arm around Mom now. She rests her head on his chest and says, "I know what you mean. But we have to go back. Dani has school and then there's Jena's appointment."

Pause to insert Dad's disappointment. He sighs. "You're right. I guess we'll just have to enjoy it while we can."

Then all of a sudden, he kicks up a little snow that crashes into my knee. Most of it is the gross, harder stuff that was on the ground before.

Everyone laughs. I roll up some snow into my palm, while Mom does not yell at me for doing so gloveless, and aim it at Dad's chest.

My father holds back in a lot of ways. He doesn't always say what he's thinking and when he does, he expects to get shot down. But snowball fights are his forte and "This means war," he declares.

We pelt limp balls of snow at one another, laughing and making idle threats. Somehow Mom gets involved and aims a few well-placed shots at Dad's head. It is two against one, and we are all too scared to involve Jena. We might if Mom weren't here. To associate yourself with any one of Jena's ailments—in this case, if she got hurt or ended up with a cold—is a bit of a suicide wish.

I hear her laugh when someone gets hit, the creaking of her smile, her heavy, loud breathing, even with my back to her, and I remember what I am fighting for. I want her here. More than anything. More than being here myself.

I shape a giant ball of snow that makes Mom laugh and tell Dad he'd better look out. Dad glances up and searches for something to duck behind.

This snowball has more new snow than the ones I've made before, so it won't hit its target and fall flaccidly to the ground; it will melt against coats and shoes and hair and knees. This snowball takes a long time to make, building an air of anticipation as Dad starts throwing smaller ones at me, to scare me from going after him. This snowball is heavy, not light, as I finally pick it up off the ground and prepare to use it. This snowball goes up, high, a world of white against the blue of the sky, up, up, up, over my head and backwards to where she is.

This snowball makes everyone freeze temporarily and then she shrieks and goes, "You cow, Dani!"

And a million little snowballs start flying at me. From Jena and Dad and even Mom, who has forgotten that she did not pray for snow—she prayed for something else.

And these snowballs make me giggle for the first time in a long time. They make me shriek and they sting and the tips of my fingers ache and I remember for the first time in a long time that I am here. Not dead or dying or waiting to die; not passing time as I wait for the people I love most in the world to drop one by one by one.

I don't know how long I'll stay, or anybody else for that matter.

But I am. Here.

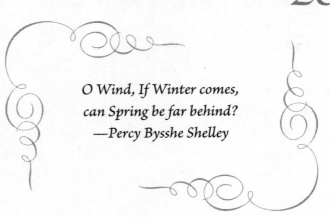

28

O Wind, If Winter comes,
can Spring be far behind?
—Percy Bysshe Shelley

The drive back home is better than the one from it. Happy is a clichéd word to use, but we are closer to it than not.

While Dad drives and Mom goes back and forth between us and him, Jena and I hang out. We play several games of cards. I forgot what a sore loser she was, and she says she forgot what a gloating winner I was.

We watch TV. No game shows today. We watch some Animal Planet documentaries and a reality show about a divorced couple living together. It's completely tacky. We can only stand it because the man is hot and doesn't speak much, and the woman's confessionals to the camera are super dishy and inappropriate.

It's a marathon, though, so when their voices become

grating, we mute them out and make up dialogue for them. This is amusing for about an episode and then Jena falls asleep underneath her six blankets, and I steal the Jena Book from where she left it, beside the couch.

It's nothing like I expect. Each entry starts with the date and then a detailed entry of what she ate that day, how she felt, when and how much medication she took. I'm just about to close it when the back cover flips open and I see that, going backwards, Jena has been drawing in it. Upon closer examination, I recognize that these are comics. Characters with names like Captain Spearhead and Villain Vikon fill the pages. It crosses my mind that this must be a code between Mom and her. They leave messages, coded inscriptions that nobody else would understand.

I wonder if I am Villain Vikon.

"They're good, aren't they?" Mom says, sitting on the arm of my couch since Jena is spread out across it and I only just have enough room to sit. "Don't tell her I said that, though," she whispers, with a shake of her head. "She does it to piss me off. Here I am trying to keep official records of what her days are like and she takes up half the pages of each book, drawing little superheroes."

Mom tugs down the blanket, where Jena's foot sticks out. "She's showing me who's boss." Even though Mom is smiling, I get the sense that it's something that actually drives her crazy, the way so much about Jena used to. The way she'd lazily throw her hair into a ponytail every single day. The way she never cleaned her room and left her door wide open, so Mom never went a day without seeing it, but then kept skulls and the NO ENTRY sign on her door, denying my mother permission to enter and fix things, the way she always wanted to.

They compromise because they have to now, but maybe deep down inside, they are still the same people I know and love. Maybe they'll come back soon and tell me stories of where they've been and what they've seen and I'll tell them too and everything will be okay.

We pull into town in all our RV-relaxed glory, an ethereal feeling of togetherness and vitality and our own non-LSD-inspired, seventies version of "everythinggunnabearite, man." *God sent snow, Mom thinks, and He's got a whole lot more resources where that came from.*

I single-handedly repaired this family over a weekend, Dad thinks. Maybe finally my wife will stop holding against me all the other ways I've failed, projects I haven't finished, and kids I can't save.

The sun is setting when we get home, an orange-red tinge painted carelessly across the sky by those angel friends of my mother's, the ones she's sure are keeping Jena alive.

We all help bring in stuff from the RV, and I shrug off Dad's coat, which I've kept ever since ice-fishing.

Jena looks tired but fine, and we're all set to continue our RV vacation right here at home.

After we're unpacked—in the loosest sense of the

word—Jena and I battle our tofu dinner by ourselves. Mom is doing laundry, while Dad is upstairs.

"I think," Jena is saying, "you and Jack would make an adorable couple."

"You know who we haven't talked about lately? Rufus."

If Jena notices my stepping around the subject of Jack, she overlooks it, opting to glare at me instead.

Right then, Mom appears in the doorway, walking into the kitchen and dishing up a plate for herself, then heading to the table.

"Jena, why's it taking you so long to eat?" Mom glances at my plate. "Have either of you even touched your food?"

"We thought we were supposed to wait for you," I lie. "Where's Dad?"

It's then I notice Mom's splotchy face, the red around the rims of her eyes.

"What's wrong?" Jena asks before I can.

"Nothing," Mom sniffs, pushing her fork into her food and bringing it up to her mouth.

"Mom, we're not stupid. We can *see* something is wrong."

At least it's not with Jena, I think.

Ignoring her, Mom points her fork at me. "Dani, we had a voicemail from the Whitaden people. You booked the commercial."

The dining room is completely quiet except for Mom's chewing, which sounds harsh and vigorous. I realize she's mad, not upset.

"Congratulations, honey," Mom says, as if suddenly remembering what she just told me. "Jena, say congratulations to your sister."

Jena's lips don't budge; neither do her eyes, which are fixed on Mom.

When I got a non-speaking part in *Oliver!* three years ago, Mom called Aunt Tish to tell her the happy news. Now I've booked my first commercial, and she looks robotic. I'm not offended; I'm worried.

We finish our food in silence—that is, those of us that do. Some of us are well-schooled in the art of not finishing food and not being seen by our mothers, so all we have to do is push the food around in our plates a little, wait till her focus is elsewhere—the best bet is on your sick twin sister—and scurry into the kitchen to expertly dispose of it.

We've figured out by now that Dad probably knows what it is she's angry about, so when I can, I sneak up to their room and find him. He's on his laptop checking e-mail.

"What's wrong with Mom?" I ask as soon as I see him. "Did she hear something about Jena?"

He frowns, still looking at the computer screen. "What do you mean? Isn't your sister downstairs?"

"Yeah," I say, "but when Mom came to eat, she looked like she'd been crying. And she's acting... weird."

Dad finishes typing his sentence, then rises from his chair, stretching. "I'll go and talk to her. Try not to worry. I'm sure it's nothing."

I know it's not nothing because I hear snatches of their conversation. I hear snatches of their conversation because they don't talk; they yell. Or Mom does. First she asks if he's smoking again. He must say yes, because things get even louder.

"How dare you!" she shouts from downstairs. I hear the sound of forks scraping plates and I realize she's washing dishes. I'm surprised they're not all broken by now, what with her exceeding the sound barrier and all. "After everything we've been through! I only asked you for one thing. *One thing*. And you couldn't do it."

Dad mumbles something, an apology or a grunt or maybe he's totally silent and that's just his stomach growling, because I have a feeling he's not getting any dinner tonight, inedible or not.

"Do you not *see* what it's like to be sick? Or, worse, to watch someone you love be sick? Where have you *been*, Eric?" she yells. "Am I crazy? Have I been the only one that's seeing it? Maybe it's because *I've* been here all this time, while you hid behind your work or even jumped at the chance to grocery shop just so you didn't have to see *this*."

This time I hear what Dad's saying. "That is not true, and you know it."

I feel bad for him. It's not true.

He wants to run away as much as I do, but he hasn't, yet. He tries to help—grocery shopping and even, God forbid, being stuck in a car with me, taking me to auditions or to school. Unfortunately for him, nothing he does comes close to wiping up your daughter's vomit or seeing her writhe in pain or going to appointment after appointment where they just want to keep trying stuff and refuse to meet your eye and tell you that it's not working.

It's not enough.

"What do you want me to do?" Dad is asking her.

"At this point," she says, "I don't care what you do. I can't even look at you."

Vigorous washing. Clanking of glass against glass. Metal against glass. Floor against glass.

"SHIT . . . Just leave it, Eric!" Scraping of glass. Fingers against glass. "I swear to God, Eric, if you get sick, I *will* leave you. I'm not going to sit here and watch you die, too. I won't. Not when you couldn't do the *one thing* I asked you to."

Watch you die too.

She mutters angry words under her breath, words too obscene, words that don't fit in her new evangelical Christian mouth.

The one thing she asked him to do was quit smoking.

And she said "too."

"And by the way, I don't know what you want to do with your coat, but right now it's out on the back porch."

I hear Dad's footsteps as he walks across the kitchen and out onto the back porch. I slip out and through the front door, then walk around the house to the porch, where Dad stands dejected, looking at the sleeve of his coat.

He jumps as I approach. "Hey, kiddo. What are you doing out here? It's cold out and you're not wearing a coat."

Light snowflakes float to the ground, a few getting caught in Dad's hair, giving him the speckled look I imagine he'll have in another few years. Or months, if our family stays this bipolar.

"Why didn't you tell her it wasn't you?" I ask, staring at the burned edge of his coat.

He shrugs. "She asked if I was smoking and I wasn't going to lie to her. *You* weren't smoking, were you?"

I shake my head. "It got burned when we were making fires, with Jack and stuff."

He runs a hand through his hair and sighs. "I should never have started up again. No matter how . . . no matter how bad things got." *"Hopeless" is what he wanted to say. "Fucked up" would do, too.*

"I'm sorry, Dad."

He shakes his head and forces a smile. "I'll tell you what. When you're rich and famous, the official Whitaden spokesperson, you buy me a brand-new coat. To make up for this."

I give him a small smile as he puts the coat around my shoulders.

"Remember the little people when you're a big star."

"Dad." I roll my eyes. "In, like, a year I'm going to destroy all footage of that commercial. And nobody will ever miss it."

My father laughs. "Maybe," he says. "But your mother doesn't need to know that."

29

Despite my parents (Mom) being a little chilly toward each other (Dad), and obsessing sort of compulsively (Mom) over certain others (Jena), this week is a good one.

Monday, it turns out, is the day our assignments are due, and while Lauren appears frazzled and totally disheveled—apparently, she was up all night finishing hers—she is happy to see me. And despite things being a tad awkward at first, Jack is, too.

Mr. Halbrook says we can hand in our assignments any time before the end of the day, so the three of us stay in during lunch and "touch up" the assignment. Mostly, Lauren sleeps with her head on the desk and Jack reads aloud all the work he's spent four weeks doing.

I tell him how terribly impressed I am.

He flushes, but seems pretty happy about it.

We still have the rest of lunchtime so we just sit there and make idle conversation—sort of like when we went ice-fishing on Saturday, but without the awkward relatives. Or the me-stomping-on-his-heart thing.

Maybe Jack and I will be friends. Or.

He tells me my family is different than he always imagined it would be, which I assume is a backhanded compliment, while I assure him that his family is exactly what I thought it would be like. If I'd ever given any real thought to the matter.

His father has been in a wheelchair for the past eighteen months, after getting into a car accident that resulted in a serious spinal cord injury. His mother works two jobs—she works at the museum downtown during the day and teaches art classes at the community college in the evenings. Jack helps out in the museum sometimes.

"So what you told me about your dad," I say, then swallow because I'm about to give *advice* and it tastes thick and sticky and hot in my throat. "You should probably tell him that. You said you don't like when people pretend everything is okay, so take your own advice." I feel a bit better now that I've said it, but it still tastes like drinking hot water when you're super thirsty. Wrong and gross and I shouldn't be giving advice. I should just refer him to Harry-with-an-*i*.

"You're right," Jack says. "I have to work up the courage first, though. That's another thing I'm not so good at." He grins wryly at the last sentence.

Something I haven't thought about in weeks pops into my mind. "I have a question for you."

"What is it?" he asks.

"That night at the party. Were you the one that drove me home?"

"Um," Jack stares down at the desk. "Yeah. I didn't think you should ... I mean, I wasn't sure you'd get home all right if I didn't."

"You saved me. I guess that makes you my hero." For the full effect of making Jack Penner uncomfortable, and making him wish I'd get struck down by lightning or polio or something, I should turn to him and bat my eyelashes, grinning mischievously. But, today, I guess I'm doing things halfheartedly.

Surprisingly, Jack laughs. "You're the only one strong enough to save yourself."

"What does that mean?"

He shrugs. "I don't know. I mean, I think you like getting into trouble. Like, a *lot* of trouble."

I frown and stare at him, letting him know he treads in volatile waters.

"You won't stop until you're ready. And you're sort of the only one who can determine that and pull yourself out."

Neither of us says anything for a second, as Lauren stirs at her desk, turning her head and falling asleep again.

"So can I write my name on our paper?" I ask Jack.

"Well, I already printed it. See, it has both of our names."

"I see that. And very good job. With, like, the fonts and the border and all that." I take the stapled pile of papers from his hand. "I just want my role in this assignment to be clear from page one."

One of Jack's eyebrows skitters up. "Okay, sure."

"Crap. My parents took away my school supplies." I hold out my hand. "Can I borrow a red pen? And blue and black, too, please."

"Your parents what?" Jack hands me the requested items, which I quite frankly consider pocketing and running away with. Red, blue, and black. The official rainbow of school pens. This far into the school year, nobody has all three colors anymore, and I don't even have one. Would he really ask me to give them back?

"Took away my school supplies: you know, stationery, writing materials. They did food and accommodation a few weeks ago. The school supplies were the only way they could really get me below the belt after my behavior."

He stares at me, a look of disbelief plastered on his face. I don't think he really believes me and I am tempted to applaud. *Bravo, Jack. You might almost know me.*

"Don't worry. What I did was really awful. I deserved it." I start to write my name in bubble letters on our cover page. Halbrook does not appreciate color; he likes varying mixtures of black and white, the different shades of gray in history. But I will make him a believer yet. Besides, Jack probably did such a great job on this assignment, it won't even matter.

"Next they'll probably take away all my clothes." I throw a wink in Jack's direction.

He laughs and the ever-faithful flush appears again. "As long as they don't take you away. You're ... er, funny."

I smile up at him. "Thanks, Jack," I say. "You're funny, too."

~

When I arrive home on the bus, Jena is drinking a hot cup of something that smells like seaweed, a new concoction Mom made for her.

Mom has been working off a lot of energy since she's busy *not* speaking to Dad and *not* laughing at any of his (admittedly) lame jokes at dinner and just generally *not* acknowledging his existence.

However, around six-thirty, I hear them talking in low, rumbling voices as Mom washes the dinner dishes and I clear the table.

As I enter the kitchen, Mom steps around me and leaves. I corner Dad. "So what, are you two married again?"

"Don't be silly. Every marriage has its ups and downs, its flows and ebbs, its—"

"Dad, please. They taught us antonyms in fourth grade."

He nudges my shoulder. "Yes, and we all know how well you listen in school." He laughs at his own joke, then quickly sobers as we hear Mom coming back down the stairs. "Well?" he asks her.

"It's a bad idea. I wasn't even going to go. And us both going? I don't feel comfortable with it."

Dad looks desperate. "I don't understand why. Danielle is home and Jena's been better than ever these past few days . . . Maybe she would even appreciate a little space."

Oh no you did not, Dad.

"I mean, er, *you* might appreciate a little space. From life, and the girls."

"Thanks, Father." I push past them and head back to the dining room. They talk for a few more minutes and then I hear Dad say, "Let's ask them."

"Girls?"

He comes into the dining room, Mom trailing behind, her hand rubbing her temple, reluctant.

"I'll live with Dad. Jena can live with Mom, so it's even. It's settled."

"Danielle!" Mom gasps, hurt and surprised. Jena giggles from her seat.

"That is *not* what we wanted to talk to you about. Your mother and I are thinking of going to a Bible study tonight."

"A small group meeting. It's not Bible study."

"Right," Dad nods. "What do you think about an evening by yourselves? Or would you prefer a babysitter?"

"Or one of us to stay home?" Mom adds.

"A babysitter," I say at the same time Jena eagerly says, "An evening by ourselves!"

Everyone looks at me.

"Yeah. I really wish Ham from two doors down would watch us." Ham is a forty-year-old man that always muttered to himself when he came out to get the mail, and never had any visitors. That is, until a few months ago when the police paid him a visit and discovered he was growing some "illegal plant products," as Dad put it at the time. We haven't seen him since.

"Very funny, Dani," Dad says now. "I really don't see what the problem is, honey. They say they'll be fine, and I agree."

Mom still looks unsure, but finally sighs. "Fine. We won't be long, though. An hour and a half. Two hours at most."

"Take your sweet, sweet time," Jena singsongs. She's already looking at me, the light green of her eyes dancing. *This is going to be fun,* they say.

"If you have any problems," Mom begins, talking for thirteen minutes straight (I count) about contact phone numbers, emergency numbers, what to do if something goes wrong. Then she turns to Jena and bombards her with a million questions: Are you sure you feel all right? Tell me, now that your father isn't here. Are you sure you don't want me to stay home?

Dad's in the study when I find him. "Bible study, huh? You must have been desperate."

He laughs, fixing the collar of his new coat. "No. It's ... your mother has wanted me to go with her for a long time. I just decided it was a good time to check it out."

Now it's my turn to laugh. "Right."

"Take care of your sister, Dani," Dad says as we head into the hallway. Mom walks toward us, finally ready to leave.

"I will. Bye, Mom! Bye, Dad!"

"See you soon, my precious stones."

Jena and I try to act as precious as possible until the front door shuts and they're on the other side of it. Then we turn to each other with fraternal-identical mischievous looks. "So," she says, "what do we do first?"

30

First, we walk to the convenience store ten minutes away and load up on as much junk food as our detoxed bodies can possibly consume in one night. Next, we walk to the park we used to play at all the time, slurping on hot frothiccinos and eating Twizzlers. The combined taste is a waxy-caffeinated-foamy-colorated mess that is entirely appropriate for this kind of night and for our first exposure to sugar (minus Harry-with-an-*i*'s M&M's) since Mom forced this abstinence upon us.

Jena has a harder time downing it than I do, and abandons her half-full frothiccino in the nearest garbage can upon entry into the park.

This time of day, the park is dark and shadowy, with rustling trees that look like mounds of blackness and light floating up from the ground, the glow of relatively fresh snow against the world above it.

We head to the swings, which are much too small for us. We look like we crashed a toy park, oversized kids in a world too small to contain us.

"Want me to push you?" I ask Jena.

She shakes her head, her too-long legs stretched far from her body. She stands, moving backwards with the swing behind her, then launches herself forward, swinging high, higher, higher, and coming back down.

High, higher, higher, and home again.

As she floats beside me, I propel myself up, too, and swing beside her. We're not exactly in sync and not quite out of sync, either. We're somewhere in the middle, drifting above this world that isn't enough for us, ignoring the shaking, the quivering of the metal rail that holds the swing.

Jena comes to a stop first.

"Once upon a time," she says, "there was a bird named Morris."

I bring myself to a full stop, too, and dig my feet into the ground, trying to find grass. "Morris was the only bird in his entire flock that couldn't sing."

"Is 'flock' right? A flock of birds?" Jena wonders out loud. "Damn, I need to get back to school."

We laugh. I take a sip of my now lukewarm drink.

"He could rap, though. He was the best rapper in his entire flock."

"One day," I continue, "he went before Congress to put forth his case. End discrimination against rapping birds."

Jena giggles. "The other birds wouldn't hear the case. They threw it out."

"Um," I frown, "why would they do that? These are

~ 206

progressive birds. And where am I supposed to take this story now?"

"I don't know. I think it went downhill when he was named Morris." She stands up. "Wanna make snow angels?"

I stand. "The snow's not deep enough."

"So?" She's already lying on the ground behind the swings, sliding her legs and arms across the snow.

"I used to think when you made a snow angel, real angels came down and slept in the space."

"Really?" Jena breathes.

"True story," I tell her, lying down on the ground now, a few feet away. I spread my arms and feet, making a hole in the snow for an angel.

We're staring up at the sky, saying nothing, when all of a sudden Jena sneezes loudly. Like, thunder-loud.

"Holy *shit*," I whisper, kicking her.

She laughs. "SORRY."

"Stop yelling," I kick her shin again.

"I SAID SORRY. AND BACK AWAY FROM THE SOC-CER SHINS. THEY ARE MY MOST PRIZED POSSESSION."

"Jena, I swear, I will *sit* on your shins if you don't stop yelling. And I weigh twice what you weigh."

"NO, YOU DON'T. AND RESPECT THE SOCCER SHINS."

I sit up, serious-faced, my hands in tight fists just to keep the threat of damage to her SOCCER SHINS alive, but I end up giggling myself and shaking my head.

"WHY ARE YOU LAUGHING?" she yells.

"Because you are an idiot," I whisper.

"I CAN'T HEAR YOU."

"Everybody in the world can hear you."

"STOP TALKING TO YOURSELF. IT'S CREEPY."

"Can you really not hear me or are you just pretending?"

"DANIELLA! SPEAK UP! I'M OLD AND DEAF."

"I've missed you, Jenavieve," I whisper too quietly for her to hear.

She sneezes again. "SERIOUSLY, TALK UP." Her voice echoes and bounces around us, sound particles crashing into one another and falling back at us.

"When do you think Mom and Dad will be home?"

"WHAT'S THAT, DANIELLA?"

"WHEN DO YOU THINK MOM AND DAD WILL BE HOME? THERE IS SNOW ON YOUR COAT AND YOUR FACE IS RED AND YOU'LL TAKE FOREVER TO REACH NORMAL BODY TEMPERATURE SO MAYBE WE SHOULD GO."

Pause.

"God, there's no need to yell," Jena says, sitting up.

I follow suit and turn to look at her. "We have an hour still before they're home. So . . ." My voice trails off. "There's something under your nose."

It's a small black blip at first, tiny, like a bug or even a piece of dark snow. But, slowly, it's melting, traveling down, and my head starts to reel as I realize what it is.

Jena knows, too. She touches her finger to it, tries to catch it, but her hands are only so big and it just keeps coming and coming and then it crosses her lips and trickles down her chin and it's on the top of her coat and I can't move.

"Oh, God," she says. "Do you have Kleenex or something?"

Nothing.

We don't need Kleenex. A little square piece of tissue will not clean up the fountain gushing out of her nose, spilling out onto the beautiful white carpet and slipping under the new snow and into the cracks in the old snow.

My fingers tremble and my brain can't think and I need to do something.

Jena has her head tipped back.

Do I move her or keep her here, where the cold will seep into her clothes and make her bleed all out? What did Mom say? What does Mom do?

"Dani, you have to run home and get my medicine. The one in the kitchen, by the spoons."

My head is shaking, whipping from left to right, but I'm up, hovering over her. "I won't go without you."

"I'll be fine," she says. "I promise. This has happened before. Just hurry, okay?"

I won't go without you. And I say it again and again and again in my head, even as I turn around and leave her kneeling with her head tipped up and her hands cupping her nose, looking up to heaven and appealing to God, just like my parents are tonight. We didn't think we'd have to join them.

Please please please please please. I sputter prayers without beginnings and words with no meaning as I sprint toward home. Heart pumping against chest, lungs expanding, expanding, expanding. Tonight I am an athlete. Me and my running shins. When I get home, I find the pills where Jena said they'd be.

Then I pick up the phone and dial 911.

I hurry back, praying I'm not too late.

Nobody bleeds like that, and it's not normal and it's happened before but not like that and why did I let her come out tonight? Why why why?

I find her huddled in the snow, her chin up to her knees, her eyes weak, tired. She's not dead, she tells me with a laugh. She just got cold.

I'm trying to give her the medicine when we hear the sirens heading this way.

"You called the paramedics?"

My hands are still shaking as I kneel next to her, begging them to hurry. "Hey, don't cry," my sister says. "I'm okay. I promise. I'm just tired."

My brain bleeds out onto the white carpet, too, leaving more red on our patch of crimson. Why did I go home? I should have gone to someone's house and called for help. They would be here by now.

Her eyelids look heavy.

Oh God, oh God, oh God.

The sirens are here. The man is sweeping her up in one fluid movement. Jena Baby almost fits in the crook of his arm.

She was not too big for the kid playground, for the wet, icy swing and the weak metal frame. I was.

As they hurry her into the ambulance, I skirt behind. I want to throw myself into a pile of snow, stuff it into my ear holes and my nostrils and swallow mouthfuls of it so I choke. I want to fill my eyes with it, tuck it in behind my eyeballs, the corners of my eyelids.

I shouldn't have brought her here.

I don't want to watch this.

I don't want to see this part and know that I did it.

I don't want to live if she doesn't.

Something is wrong and the man carrying her is stopping, turning around. "Where's her sister?"

I don't answer, but they pull me forward to Jena. I am the girl who's covered in blood, who's drowning in her tears and choking on her words.

Suddenly, I'm in the ambulance with her, while they try to keep her eyes from closing.

"Dani," she says too loud. "Dani?"

"She's right here," somebody says for me. They give me a push forward.

"You're here. Good." She grabs one of my fingers, the only one I dared to hold near the stretcher they've placed her on. "It's not your fault. Don't think that. And if you do something stupid, I'm going to be so pissed at you."

What stupid thing would I do?

What thing stupider (than this)?

Does she mean I should stop thinking about bursting open the doors in this cramped ambulance and throwing myself out? Does she mean not going back home, lying in the bottom of the pool and this time leaving the cover on so nobody finds me until it's too late?

"I'm sorry," I whisper. Those are the only words I can cough up, and they are not enough.

"Don't be. Stop it," she says. "Just stay with me, okay? Don't do anything stupid."

I don't want to stay with you.

I want to hide under the tires of this ambulance and let them peel me off the road.

"Okay," I mumble. And she smiles.

I give her more of my hand, three more bloodstained fingers.

Somebody says something to me about staying strong and contacting our parents. We pull up at the hospital.

Then they're wheeling Jena somewhere and I'm running alongside, no idea where we're going, but here, because I made her a promise.

And all I can think about is snow angels and the little craters we made for them to land in when they come to Earth. Hers is covered in red now: colored, warm bits of snow that will stain the angels that sleep in them.

Maybe the ones we made tonight were different. Maybe angels don't sleep in them after all.

Shallow graves for dead angels.

31

This night secretly weaves in hours and hours from other days, until it feels much longer than just one.

Even though I can't hold Jena's hand all night, I stay in the waiting room with Dad, while Mom does.

She still has her Bible from Bible study and she reads it beside my sister's bed, her lips moving occasionally, pleading, praying.

They didn't cast stones at me or curse the day I was born. They only hugged me and let me cry into their shoulders and told me it wasn't my fault.

"I'm going to get some coffee. Want anything?" asks Dad.

"No, thanks."

"Sure?" Dad asks. "Well, we should be heading home in a bit anyway."

"I told Jena I'd stay here."

His eyebrow rises. "Dani, you need to get some rest. We can stop by first thing tomorrow morning."

"Okay?" Dad asks, when I don't say anything.

"Okay."

After he gets coffee and goes in to see Mom again, Dad comes out and tells me it's time to go. Jena is "just resting" right now, so there's no reason why I can't come by and see her tomorrow. It's all settled.

I don't sleep at all. It keeps replaying in my mind over and over again. The bad parts, mostly. The part where the blood fills up her hand and starts to drip between her fingers. The part where I come back and she's so small I can hardly make her out in the shadows. The part where she closes her eyes and sleeps, while doctors schedule more tests and wonder aloud whether this is it, whether the countdown begins now.

And if it is, did I say enough? Why don't I ever say or do enough?

I feel like unzipping my skin and crawling out of it, tearing off the bits that stick and burning them.

I have *four* lives. Why did I wait for this?

How did I let this happen?

I picture her in the park again, in the hospital, dying.

I let her.

I let her.

I let her.

We wake up late and Dad offers to call the school and tell them I'll be absent, so we can go and see Jena. He just got off the phone with Mom, who says she is awake and better.

I tell him thanks, but no thanks, big day today, don't want to miss any more (I've already missed math), can I see her after school?

He's a little surprised but agrees. While Dad drives, he says, "I really hope you're not still beating yourself up over last night. That could have happened anywhere. It *would* have happened anywhere."

"I shouldn't have taken her out, though."

"Why not?" Dad cuts off the engine in front of my school. "Because she's sick, she shouldn't get to hang out with her sister, eat too much sugar, and laugh? She shouldn't get to go outside and play, remember why she likes living and why she needs to keep fighting?"

His voice is impassioned and as I look at him, expressionless, he catches himself and sighs. "I guess I've been wanting to say that for a while. I hate that things are this way, Dani. But you know what? We still have each other. We're all still here. It's not over yet."

I move to open my door.

"It's not," Dad says again.

"Will you be out here at three?"

"Three-oh-five," he says. "Isn't that the official end?"

Dad is finally catching on, but we're all too worn out to care. "Yeah. Bye."

He waits till I'm inside to drive off. I wait till he's driven off to come back out.

How did I let this happen?

I walk to the bus stop a couple of blocks from the school.

The bus is taking forever to come and, when I grow tired of waiting, I just start walking. There's a trail through Haneson Park that leads up the mountain. The higher up you go, the more you can see of the town below and everything looks like a toy model. You can't tell houses from churches from schools.

Two middle-aged women power walk past, and the jogger behind me is gaining on me. I pause for a moment and then start to go in the opposite direction, climbing downhill. It isn't nearly as high or as steep here, but at least there are fewer people.

Tears blur my vision when I finally stop, when I approach the ledge.

As I stand there, I whisper a prayer. Or maybe it's more of an order. I say, "Jena needs this one more than I do."

This one.

Please, please *give it to her.*

And then I stumble forward and let myself fall. Faster, faster, faster.

I know I promised her I wouldn't do this. But I'm not strong enough to watch her die. I'll do it nine times before I let her do it once.

It's the only thing I can think of to do.

I hear a shout, a stranger's voice above me.

My last thought as I plummet to my death is this:

Six down, three to go.

three

32

When you die, does your life flash before your eyes?

Does it happen so fast that you can't pick out one memory from the other, or do the moments stick out, good, bad, beautiful, ugly, before, after?

If you don't like what you see, can you ask for a refund?

Do you know you're dying?

Is there opportunity for regrets or do you have to suck up the fact that This Is Your Life?

Is there somebody waiting to receive you on the other end?

If you change your mind, is there a Panic button you can press?

Do you taste your favorite foods, smell your favorite smells, hear your favorite sounds, one last time?

Does everything you've ever wondered just suddenly start to make sense?

Can you convey telepathic messages to the person you want to find you?

Do you get to tick Ghost or Away From Here, Please?

Are you detached from your body, watching people react, and getting to bring bad luck on the people who aren't devastated by your death?

Does it hurt to die?

Do you get to meet the angels that slept in your angel-craters?

Do you get to meet God?

Is He happy to see you, or disappointed?

Can you send help to the people you've left behind?

What if they really, really need it?

Can you watch them while they're sleeping, far enough away that it's not creepy, but close enough that they feel you and don't feel so alone?

Isn't there a way you can make them understand, help them forgive you?

The answer to all these things is no. But you have to die to know that. Really die. And then, you don't come back.

33

Voices swarm around me, but everything is black. Any minute now, I'll wake up and have to explain.

I think I'm in a hospital. I can hear people shouting orders, bustling around me, but I don't feel anything.

It seems like I died bad this time. This is the first time my fingers don't tingle and my throat doesn't burn and my skin doesn't itch. My body feels detached from itself, frozen.

I can't move.

I start counting Mississippis.

Fifteen Mississippis.

One hundred Mississippis. Two hundred Mississippis.

I try to force my eyelids apart, but everything remains black.

I can't wake up.

Suddenly, I start to panic. This is not what it feels like to die; I don't remember it like this. Usually, it is one moment of pitch black before the light bursts through, whether I want it to or not.

Now there is only black.

"I told you not to do anything stupid, you stupid cow." Jena. She's close to me; I can feel it. But I can't feel myself.

Jena! I try to form the word, but I can't. The silence is hollow and empty, and it ricochets off the voices of people without faces around me.

One of those voices is my mother's. She is not calling me a stupid cow, although I suspect she might want to. It's hard to understand what she's saying at first, but then I realize she's praying. For me.

I'm confused, but mostly angry, because these prayers belong to Jena. These prayers for life and healing are not, and should not be, for me. My sister needs them more than I do.

I try to inhale, and I finally, finally, feel something. A sharp stab of pain pounds down on my chest, making it impossible to breathe.

As my mother continues to spew prayers, ones that surprise me with their depth, that sound like she really believes them as she prays, I start yelling, screaming at her to stop.

To make it stop, *make it stop, make it stop.*

If she is keeping score, and I think she is, then she has to know that I don't need her prayers. I am, I will be, fine. I'm only on my seventh life.

What if we were wrong?

I start counting.

One—the car accident.

Two—the chest infection.

Three—that time I drowned.

Four—that time with the motorcycle.

Five—that time with the pills.

Six—that time I jumped.

That's six. Six.

What if we were wrong?

I try again to speak, to scream, to move.

Nothing.

I, the girl with ~~nine~~ seven lives, am dead. Jena, the girl with one, is not.

This is what I wanted.

Isn't it?

For Jena to live at any cost.

If I die, if I die for real, will she be well? Not better, but *well*. What if this is what she has needed all along? One cat's life for the other; my life for hers?

All her words start coming back. Not my mother's; Jena's. About being each other's backups. Jena hasn't given up. *She* is fighting.

The blackness isn't going away.

I suck in a breath—a thin, short breath—and fire erupts in my chest. It hurts to breathe and I want to sleep and I want Jena to be well.

But what if I was wrong? What if I have only one life and this is it?

I suck in another breath and it stings, but it fills my body. It reminds me of a time when breathing wasn't traitorous or unfair or labored; it was just breathing. It was just what we did. It reminds me of Once Upon a Times that had endings we chose for them—happy or violent or funny or sad—or the ones that kept on going because we never could decide.

If I die now, she might have to live without me. Alone with Mom and Dad, awkward dinners with the empty fourth chair, hurting, angry, wishing she could have done more, thinking I did this because of her. She would never forgive herself. Would she ever forgive me?

If I die now, here is a period. Round, black, final. My heart stops and my lungs fail and my brain finally, finally gets to sleep.

If I die now, she might not fight. And there's no guarantee we'll go to the same place.

I breathe in, hold it longer this time, even as my chest throbs from the pain.

I want to scream and cry and yell that it's not fair *it's not fair it's not fair it's not fair it's not fair*.

It is not fair that my sister got sick and I didn't. It's not fair that I couldn't—*can't*—help her.

It's not fair that people get answers from God. They get healed, they get miracles and wonders that they might not need as much as I need this, as much as Jena needs this.

It's not fair that either choice I make could be wrong and I have no guarantees or lifelines.

It's not fair that what eats away at me, the ghosts I see in broad daylight, are weaker and smaller than me, and if I choose to fight them, I might win.

I breathe, breathe in, keep breathing. Everything hurts.

I picture waking up when she's not across the hall, not in her soccer uniform, not anywhere anyone can see her.

The throbbing gets worse, but I inhale and don't let it out.

I would do anything for Jena.

Most people think the biggest sacrifice, the greatest act of love you can give is to die for someone. And probably it is.

But sometimes it is the opposite.

The biggest thing you can do for someone is to live.

Once upon a time, I thought too long about the taste of marsh-mallows in hot, hot chocolate, the way moist sand feels between your toes, the way the sun beats down against the nape of your neck, making you wish you could unzip your skin and hide it from the sun. Summer.

I thought about waking up and wanting to, about making snow angels with sisters and whispering secrets; about mothers who embarrassed you by singing opera in the car and dads who tried a little too hard to be cool.

I thought about the lightness in your chest while you were laughing, the way your ears rang from loud music, the smell of fried food and the taste of s'mores. Bones that don't crack, but hold up by themselves. Hair that doesn't shed. Scars that heal and bruises that disappear.

Once upon a late night or an early, early morning, I thought too long about all these things.

And then I opened my eyes.

one

34

You always expect more to have changed, when you've been gone for any significant amount of time. There's something about being away that warps time, stretches it out like spandex where you least expect it and crams it close together when you're not looking.

I'm expecting it to be spring when I wake up. But it's still only almost spring, same as it was when I was lost in a snowless winter storm, and didn't notice.

As if to reassure me that this is the world I left behind— not one of those parallel universes people in movies find themselves in after a near-death experience—my first day back at school after two weeks, I arrive late, with my father by my side, helping me through the door on my crutches.

In any other scenario, it would be deeply thrilling having a man open doors for me, someone to lean on for support and to pull out my chair. Now, though, it's mortifying.

"You can go now," I whisper to him. He's holding the door open for me as I limp through. I have one of those fat leg braces, which I have to admit to being proud of. It's just a bad sprain, but it looks dramatic. And although my fractured rib is supposed to heal in the next month or so, I'm excused from gym class for the rest of the year. Mom called and worked out a nice little system in which she and Dad take turns dropping me off at Harry-with-an-*i*'s office for therapy when everyone else has gym.

I can't wait to brag about this one. While they work up a sweat and invent menstrual cramps to get out of P.E., the only time I perspire is reaching for a handful of M&M's. And, of course, transporting warehouse-sized bags of the things into the back of Dad's car—an undertaking which is entirely his these days, what with my condition. The truth is, I'm lucky I didn't get hurt more than I did.

"Hello there." Mr. Halbrook rises, putting down whatever book he was reading and walking toward us. "How are you doing, Danielle? And you must be Mr. Bailey."

"That's me." Dad sticks out his hand and shakes Halbrook's. While I force my way through, Dad and Mr. Halbrook continue to talk, presumably about me, history, or other boring stuff. The classroom is quieter than usual, with heads ducked down, pencils scratching paper. Did someone warn Halbrook ahead of time that a Parent was coming? Probably. Why else would they be doing actual work?

Jack's eyes meet mine, but I don't sit next to him because National Science Fair champion Toby, who has always had it in for me and has just been waiting for an opportunity to take my place (this just proves it), has made himself comfortable in my former seat.

I look away from Jack first and sit in the nearest empty chair. Lauren waves and smiles at me, glancing at Halbrook to ensure he didn't see before going back to her work. Clearly she's still trying to redeem herself after her brief and mildly entertaining detour into delinquency. I notice that Rachel Talbot and her trusty Fruit Roll-Up are conspicuously absent.

As Dad and my math teacher continue to talk, I pretend not to notice that more than half the class keeps glancing my way, stage-whispering about my return. I wonder what they are saying. Are they scared of me? Do they think I'm some unbalanced freak waiting to kill someone other than myself?

"So," I say, speaking above the whispers. "What's everyone been up to?"

When no one rushes to respond, I continue, just wanting to get past this awkward "the girl that tried to kill herself is back" phase. "Don't all answer at once." Silence. "Well, in that case, let me start us off. My two weeks were pretty uneventful. On Tuesday, I went—"

Dad and Mr. Halbrook are both looking at me now. My father looks slightly incredulous. All this time, he'd chalked me up as the quiet, unassuming, nondisruptive kind.

"Dani?"

"Yeah, Dad?" I turn to the girl on my left, a German exchange student. "This is my dad, everyone, by the way. I think he secretly longs to come back to high school and relive his glory days, which is why he's *still* here."

Using politics to worm his way into Halbrook's heart.

"Um, Danielle?" Mr. Halbrook interrupts. "Your classmates are in the middle of a test."

Well, that *might* explain the whispering, but I'm not convinced. "Wait. I don't have to take it, do I?"

"He means," Dad whispers, "be quiet." It's too late, though. The kids he's pleading with me not to distract are mostly all looking up from their papers, Mathistory the furthest thing from their minds.

"Actually," Halbrook says, his eyes lighting up like the next word out of his mouth should be *Eureka!*, "it is really just a short in-class essay to see how much you learned from the projects you did. Why don't you attempt it?"

"That sounds like a great idea," Dad says.

"But I haven't had a chance to prepare."

Mr. Halbrook is already making his way to his desk, picking up a piece of paper. "I want you to try it anyway. I know you missed our class discussions, but you did the assignment."

If my dad wasn't standing here, so hopeful about my *possibilities* and my *potential*, blinded by my angelic actions and noble contributions toward humanity, I might put up a larger fight with Halbrook, threaten to tell my parents or the school board or something.

Instead, I just sigh and ask to borrow a pen as a piece of paper lands in front of me.

I stare at the page, my eyes glazing over the words. None of this makes sense. And yeah, I never listen in class, but since when were we contrasting the presidencies of FDR and Lincoln? Since when was FDR president?

I stick up my hand.

"Yes, Danielle?"

"Does FDR stand for Federal Dominion of Russia?"

"What?" Both Dad and Halbrook look surprised.

It's probably a good time for my lips to start quivering. "I don't understand what any of this means."

Lauren's hand shoots up, but she doesn't wait for Halbrook to give her the okay to speak. "Am I the only one who's super distracted?"

Halbrook sighs.

"Danielle." Dad's eyes send me a warning.

My hand goes up again. Halbrook comes right to my desk this time. "What's the problem?" Then all of a sudden, "Oh! Sorry, this isn't the test. This is just a, er, draft for the book I'm working on."

"You're writing a book?"

Lauren sighs loudly and tells me to *please God* shut up. She has to do well on this.

Halbrook nods, handing me another piece of paper.

The question at the top: What did you learn from your assignment on the history of mathematics?

I sigh, shutting my eyes and tracing the bruises on my left cheek with my finger.

"Dani, come on. What are you doing?" Dad whispers beside me.

This is a nightmare. "Dad, can you please leave? There's no way I can concentrate with you here."

"You didn't even bring a pen."

"I thought," I spit, "that today might be more homecoming, less school. I don't know if you've noticed, but I'm über popular."

Dad shakes his head, looks like he's about to say something else, but finally just pats my shoulder. "Do your best, okay?"

Then he says goodbye to Mr. Halbrook, waves at Jack Penner—did I mention the part where this is a nightmare?—and stalks out of the room.

With him gone, I can safely put my head on the desk and drop the pen in my hand.

I know I'm supposed to be turning over a new leaf and everything, but this test doesn't even seem doable.

I make the mistake of opening my eyes. Jack is staring at me. For the longest time, I stare back, trying to figure out if he's telepathically communicating answers to me, or mouthing them, or why the hell he's staring at me.

I'm bruise-faced and about forty-four percent less attractive than I was the last time he saw me, so that could be it.

Maybe he's not looking at me, but through me.

He might also be wishing that the other sister came to school and this one stayed home.

I don't know what he's thinking, so I look away again.

I pick up my pen and stare at it for a while.

If I write my name, he has to give me at least one point. Maybe. I don't know why teachers don't count that. A week ago, I couldn't have written my name. Thirteen years ago, I couldn't have, either. And seventeen years ago, I didn't have one.

So the fact that I can write it, on request and under pressure, shows proof of learning. I deserve one point for that argument, if not the name.

Think, Dani. I only need one sentence. *What was the assignment about again?*

All I have to do is think up the most ambiguous statement possible, make it sound a little philosophical, add in a pinch of near-truth, and voilà.

And then, just like that, it hits me.

I pick up my pencil and write it down. It's only a few sentences, but it's *good*.

Mr. Halbrook will *eat* this up.

For good measure—and since I have a bunch of extra time—I add a special P.S. just for him.

After class, as Lauren takes my paper up to the front and I struggle to get out of my seat, Jack comes over and holds out my crutches for me.

"Hey," he says.

"Hi." I take the one crutch from him, then the other. "So, listen, if you were trying to give me hints during class, I totally suck at reading lips and I didn't get any of them. Except maybe potpourri. Was that one?"

"No."

I sigh. "Yeah, I didn't think so."

"So where . . . how have you been?" he asks as we make our way to the front of the classroom, where Lauren is holding the door open. It hasn't even occurred to her that, for my friend, she was more than a little combative in class earlier. I mean, sure, she let herself go for a while there school-wise, but we're nowhere near the end of the world. I don't think.

"Oh, you know," I mumble. I know there've been all kinds of rumors flying around about me. It wouldn't be high school if there weren't. I don't want it to be awkward, but I want to be honest. I don't know why. "Battling demons."

Jack doesn't speak right away, but when he does, he says, "Well, I'm glad you won. I knew you could."

My crutches must be pinching my underarms again, and that's why my eyes want to water.

"Thanks."

That, or PMS.

"I also," Jack says, glancing quickly at his feet, then back up again, "talked to my dad."

My eyes widen. He took *my* advice? "What did he say?"

He shrugs. "It wasn't a total bust. It felt good to talk about it, but I'll tell you later."

Right then, someone walks past me and I stare at her, trying to remember where I've seen her before. Dirty-blond hair, arms that swing exaggeratedly when she walks.

"Oh my God!" I exclaim. "Is that Candy?"

"Yeah. I guess she's no longer Goth."

My mouth falls open, not because I'm that shocked or anything, but because Candy, trying-to-be-hardcore Kandi, was an easy target. I mean, she practically invited it, just in the way she, you know, blinked. But this Candy, without the holey jeans and metal bracelets and spiked hair, means I might need to change my material. I mean, I still hate her guts, but now I need new reasons.

Why do I miss *all* the good things?

34 ½

Danielle Bailey

Q: Where did math start?
A: It's hard to tell where something starts. Beginnings are infinite, or too far away to recall. Endings are easier to find and to define. See, most people think math is about numbers and equations, but it's so much more than that, which is why classifying a start and end is so difficult. Anyway, no offense, but I'm partial to beginnings. There's something about starting that feels good, better than ending. But yeah, I don't know how math started. You'd have to ask God.

Sincerely, Dani

P.S. Congrats on writing a book, Mr. Halbrook. I always imagined you would. I just hope you don't stop teaching and go full-time, because that would be too bad.

35

It's been two months since I jumped, and Jena's back in the hospital again. She's on high-dose chemo and radiation right now, and at the end of this plan, she'll get a marrow transplant from a donor.

Not all days are good. Some days she's pasty and frail and small and I'm too weak to look at her, and other days, even if she's fine, the smell of bleach and illness and family members and residents who haven't bathed in days crowds her hospital room, pushing us into corners, often separate.

Some days, she talks about dying and I have to tell her she can't talk like that. I can say from personal experience that it sucks.

And we have a deal that she'll try not to. She'll try really really really hard. And she has. But if she fails, I have to figure out some way to forgive her. And if I fail—on the days I forget how to be strong for her—she has to figure out some way to forgive me.

We play cards or watch the game show channel. We listen to music and watch bad reality TV. I sneak in popcorn and soda, but not too much, because we're both trying to live now.

She's doing okay. Better than most people expected, and far better than I expected. It'll be a few weeks before she can come home.

I told her I wouldn't let her in. Not without her skull and crossbones, her loud, angry music that makes the house tremble, and those PRECIOUS SOCCER SHINS.

It's funny. If anyone was going to give me the silent treatment, to hold against me what I did or tried to do, I figured it would be Jena.

But my mom was the one who barely spoke or even looked at me after I got home from the hospital. She would go quiet and press her lips together until they formed a long, thin line.

Even now, she still can't quite look at me.

I don't think she's ever going to forgive me.

I'm not entirely sure whether it's for my part in what happened to Jena that night or my part in what happened to me. I've been too afraid to ask.

So I usually slip past her, carrying my plate upstairs to my room when Dad is working and Mom's home from the hospital resting, and it's just the two of us.

Tonight, though, I wake up and find a glimmer of moonlight casting shadows on my face. I went to bed early, so it's probably before midnight.

I can't get back to sleep and, after a few more unsuccessful attempts, I get up and go down to the living room.

I'm not expecting to find her there, wrapped in all of Jena's blankets, a steaming mug in her hand as she stares off into space.

I'm not expecting to hear her voice, soft and inviting in contrast to the darkness in which I hide.

"You're not sleeping," she says.

At first, I contemplate just turning around and going back to bed, because that would be easier, and I don't stay for hard things. Or so says my track record.

But this time, I dig my feet in and pull my voice out and answer. "You're not, either."

"Sometimes," Mom says, "I have trouble sleeping."

I know, I want to say, but don't.

"Usually, a cup of decaf helps. Other times, I'll read."

"Read," I repeat, as if the word is foreign. Everything else came to mind: pray, write, research, have an affair, commit crimes, play online games.

"Yes." Mom nods, a faint smile just visible with the small amount of light in here. "Dark, gory horror stories."

"They must really improve your sleep."

She laughs softly. "Sometimes, it's just good to know that someone out there has it worse. And there always is that someone."

I can't see her very well, but nonetheless my eyes are boring into the figure in front of me, puzzled, confused.

"So why aren't *you* sleeping?" Mom asks.

"I just couldn't." I realize now, standing here, that I was wrong. It's not eleven o'clock at all. It has to be the wee hours of the morning.

"Have you watched the DVD yet?" She draws a sip from her cup.

I'd forgotten all about it. The DVD we got three days ago from Whitaden, holding my one and only claim to fame: my commercial. We shot it two weeks ago. Though both the leg brace and arm cast came off last month, I wasn't exactly in peak condition and my injuries—including an unfortunate chipped front tooth—nearly cost us the job. I suspect this, too, is part of the reason Mom's been so angry. See, it turns out Whitaden doesn't take too kindly to its actors launching themselves off high places. But it does pay to have actor-turned-director friends.

"Nope. Not yet," I tell her.

There's a slight pause. "Do you want to?"

Five minutes later, we're sitting in front of the television, waiting for the DVD to start. Maybe it's her coffee or the fact that it's spring. My brain is convinced it's her nearness, her warmth, the fact that I miss my mother in more ways than I can say and I don't want her to hate me and I don't want to lose her, too. Not if I don't have to.

For some reason, I blurt this out: "I'm sorry."

For a second, I think she'll just ignore me. But suddenly, the TV goes black and she turns to me.

Mom sighs. "I'm not angry with you, Danielle. I just don't know how to express enough of the things I have to say to you."

I chew my inner lip. Nibble. Nibble. Nibble.

"There aren't guarantees on anything. I'm sure you've had plenty of time to think about this, but there are millions of ways to die. Millions and millions. And at any moment, anything could go wrong and it could all be over. For any of us."

"I just didn't want to have to watch her die anymore."

"I know," Mom says. "But she nearly had to watch *you* die."

There's a sniff and I realize Mom is holding back tears. "The hardest part of all of this is how helpless I feel. I want to take all your pain and bury it, keep it far away, where it can't reach you." *Pain-transferring voodoo, not cancer.*

I slip my arm around her. "I know."

My heart throbs and aches and, for once, it's not for myself. It's for all of us. It's for everyone who knows what it's like to be helpless, to have to watch on the sidelines, to be paralyzed, literally unable to do anything.

It's *hard.*

"She's doing good, though," Mom says, brightening a little. "Really good."

"Yeah," I agree.

"She's not like us, you know."

For a second, I think she means what I've always thought she meant—Jena wasn't in the accident and we don't know if she has nine lives. Most likely, she doesn't.

That's always what I've thought it meant. We have more, she has less.

Jena Baby's not like us.

But this time, it hits me that maybe that's not what Mom means at all.

Jena *isn't* like us. She fights and she kicks and she won't let you get away with anything. She's weak, but not defeated. Small, but not invisible. Sick, but not dead.

We're not allowed to give up.

Not yet.

Mom dabs at her eyes. "Enough of this. Ready to watch your groundbreaking debut?"

I can't help but roll my eyes. "I'd hardly call it that."

She presses the remote, and it starts.

A girl whose dragon breath socially annihilates her the first day of high school. But then, enter Whitaden. And her whole world is changed. Suddenly, she has friends, a hot boyfriend, and everything she ever wanted in life.

Whitaden. Brighten your world.

Mom claps and grins when it's over, looking proud and excited, her eyes twinkling and the crinkles beside her eyes seeming less alien on her face and more like they belong there—they look like footprints from a journey.

As Mom plays it "just one more time," I stare at the screen. At the girl with the mahogany hair, the hazel eyes, the sparkling white smile, and the newly capped tooth.

I don't know the girl in the commercial. Not the way she

cocks her head to the side and grins like her world isn't in danger of falling off its axis, of tilting from right to wrong, from up to down.

I don't know how she gets up each day and lives it.

For now, that sorry tooth is all we have in common, but I'm getting to know her.

She seems friendly enough, like she brushes her teeth and like she also appreciates a good joke.

I'm pretty sure I'll like her.

She looks a lot like my sister.

Acknowledgments

Thank you to my agent, the indomitable Suzie Townsend, for your unwavering belief in this book and in my writing. You are the very best. Margaret Ferguson, your insight and attention to detail are unmatched. Thanks for your hard work and for transforming *All These Lives* from a manuscript into a real, live book.

Thanks to Meredith Barnes, Sara Kendall, and Jacqueline Murphy. Thanks also to Susan Dobinick and the fabulous team at Farrar Straus Giroux.

Dr. Golsteyn and Dr. Sheila Pritchard, thank you so much for sharing your expertise with me. Any mistakes are all mine.

Many thanks to every one of my writing friends: Jeanette Schneider and Suzanne Hayze. Lisa and Laura Roecker, for braving through that early draft. Mariah Irvin, because who else would I talk misbehaving celeb assistants, good books, writing, and life with? Shannon Messenger, your enormous talent is matched only by your heart. Serenity Bohon, thank you for caring about the little and the big things, and for teaching me to do the same.

Thank you to my blog readers, for finding my corner of the Web and coming back. I like you better than a million Twizzlers.

I get to share 2012 with the über-talented Apocalypsies. The world doesn't have my permission to end this year; I can't wait to read all your books.

Thanks to Ms. Eck and Mrs. Matteoti, who taught me to love words. Mrs. Enslin, thank you for everything, especially the butterfly clips.

A big thank-you to all my family and friends. Bek, for realizing how long forever is. Kate, I'm blessed to know you.

Thank you to my mom and dad. I'll probably never know how much you've given. I love you, always.

Thank you to my extraordinary sisters. The jury is still out on the whole multiple lives thing. But if, somehow, we got to do this whole thing again, I'd a) demand supreme cartwheeling abilities, and b) pick you and you and you. Every time. Not because we have the same (questionable) sense of humor. Not because you're always game for a Twizzler run . . . or three. Not because you told me to keep going, to always keep going, and this book would still be five pages long without you. Not because—but that, too. I love you, you know. And I'm only slightly resentful that you're all taller.

God, thank You for blessing me beyond words. Thank You for never letting go.